KNIGHT

SILVER SAINTS

FIONA DAVENPORT

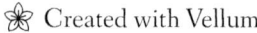 Created with Vellum

KNIGHT

SILVER SAINTS MC

Shane "Knight" Ballard knew the blonde beauty he saw on the courthouse steps was meant to be his. But with danger looming, the time wasn't right to claim her. Not when it could put her safety at risk.

What Knight didn't know was that Kiara Timkins was already smack-dab in the middle of it all. The crooked judge the Silver Saints were looking into was her father...and she was going to need Knight to come riding to her rescue.

PROLOGUE

I ran a hand over my head, and the buzz-cut hairs prickled my skin as I watched the large wooden double doors that led to Judge Timkins' courtroom.

Any minute, Rom, one of my brothers in the Silver Saints Motorcycle club, would be strolling out without the metal bracelets he'd been sporting earlier that morning.

He'd been in Devil's Jesters' territory recently to deliver something to a friend when the cops showed up because of a "tip." Since he didn't even have his own registered weapon on him, he gave them permission to search his bike, and whaddya know, they found a stolen gun.

The cops were too fucking scared of the Jesters to do any investigating, so they just took Rom in.

When they finally got around to doing their fucking jobs—or at least, their lazy-ass version of it—the security tapes for the bar had been erased.

They didn't count on Hack—another brother and a world-class hacker—recovering the footage, or our fixer, Dom, "finding" proof that the gun had been stolen by a Jester in a home invasion a few days before Rom was picked up.

His lawyer, Gary Finch—a slimy asshole, but the only one we'd had to deal with this bullshit—had assured me that the evidence we provided to prove Rom's innocence was solid.

Considering it showed a rival MC planting a stolen weapon in my brother's saddlebag, most people would assume that was enough to have the bullshit charges against Rom dropped. But he'd been assigned to a dirty judge. Which was how his misdemeanor became a felony, even with a clean record. On top of that, the judge managed to keep Rom from his phone call, handed over fake papers that waived his right to a hearing, and had Rom staring down ten years in prison.

We figured that gaining the evidence for Rom would expose the judge, but it ended up becoming two separate issues. So while I handled delivering the papers to get Rom's ass out of jail, Doc—the

club's fixer—and his old lady, Oakley, were dealing with the dirty judge.

The doors opened, drawing me from my thoughts, and I lifted my chin to Rom's lawyer, Gary Finch. I didn't like the asshole, but we'd paid him enough to earn his loyalty—for this job, anyway—and he'd worked hard to clear my brother. And his lack of morals came in handy from time to time when the lawyer we preferred to use wouldn't compromise his. Not that we'd ever asked him to, or he wouldn't work with us.

Rom followed Gary, and when he spotted me, he headed in my direction.

"Brother," I grunted as we shook hands and clapped each other on the back.

"Thanks," he grunted back. Then we walked to the large set of stairs that led to the lobby and silently descended.

Rom waited until we were outside before he spoke again. Too many ears in the courthouse. "You find out who put in the tip?"

I nodded. "Mac figured you'd want to deal with the piece of shit."

"Damn straight."

Rom said something else, but I didn't have a

fucking clue what it was because something else captured my attention.

Golden waves shimmered in the sunshine as they bounced around the shoulders of the most gorgeous woman I'd ever seen. She had a sweet face with high cheekbones, and a rosebud mouth spread in a happy smile.

Her body was the opposite of her face, though. It was made for sin. Full and curvy in all the right places. My pants grew snug as my eyes devoured her big tits, round hips, and the thick thighs I wanted to bury my face between.

Suddenly, her head turned, and for a second, our eyes met. She was too far for me to see the color of her eyes, but her incredible smile was aimed at me. Then she looked away, breaking the connection. But that one second changed everything.

The light around her was probably just a trick of the sunlight, but it seemed more like a glow of innocence. It probably should have sent me running in the opposite direction. My life was full of darkness, and I had no business corrupting an angel.

It wasn't going to stop me, though.

Now wasn't the time to go after her, but as soon as all this bullshit was handled, her pretty little ass was mine.

1

My first semester at college turned out to be a lot harder than I'd expected. Although I was an art major, all but one of my classes fulfilled my general education requirements, so it felt like high school all over again. Only much harder.

It also didn't help that I was homesick. I'd been so excited to move away from home—and "spread my wings" as my mom liked to put it—but I had been ready to come back home for a visit after the first month. Unfortunately, my classes had kept me too busy for trips to see my parents as often as I wished I could. I'd barely made it back for Thanksgiving. The trip before that, I'd only been able to pop in quickly for a couple of days, and I stopped to have lunch with my dad at the courthouse on my way out of town since it felt as though I'd barely seen him while I was there.

Now that winter break was finally here, I had a whole month to spend with them. After pulling my Mini Cooper—a high school graduation present from my dad—into the garage, I jumped out and raced into the house. I was so excited to be back that I left all my stuff in the car and headed straight for the kitchen. "Mom, I'm home!"

"Shh, keep it down." She lifted her wineglass toward the hallway that led to my dad's office before taking a healthy gulp. "Your father is working from home today."

My brows drew together. "Really? I saw his car in the garage, but I figured you dropped him off today or something. I thought I'd have to go to the courthouse to see him if I didn't want to wait until tonight."

"You definitely won't find him there today." She polished off the rest of her wine and poured another glass. "Or anytime soon, for that matter."

I blinked a few times as I moved closer, my excitement quickly turning to concern. My mom had wine with dinner every night, but I couldn't remember ever seeing her drink during the day by herself. My dad being at home was just as strange since it was the middle of the day during the week. He should have been busy presiding over a case. "What's going on?"

"Nothing, dear." She dropped the empty wine bottle in the recycling bin. "Everything is fine, just like it always is."

She didn't sound very convincing. Her high-pitched tone was the same fake one she used when talking to someone she didn't like but felt she needed to impress. "Then why are you having a liquid lunch? And what's Dad doing at home when he should be at the courthouse?"

"Those damn bikers have driven me to drink," she muttered.

My eyes widened as my head reared back. My mom hardly ever used swear words, and I didn't think she had any clue motorcycle clubs existed. She didn't watch the same shows as I did, and the people she hung out with were more likely to drive a Rolls-Royce than a motorcycle. "Bikers?"

"Your father went up against a local biker gang during his last case." She rolled her eyes with a huff. "And he failed miserably."

Staring at the bottle of wine she was opening, I wondered if it was the alcohol talking. "That doesn't make any sense. How could Dad lose? He doesn't try cases; he's a judge."

"No, he *was* a judge."

I felt a sinking sensation in the pit of my stomach. "What do you mean?"

"He's been suspended from the bench."

My chest tightened as I shook my head. "I don't understand. Everything was fine the last time I visited. How could all of this have happened in such a short time?"

"It feels like forever to me," she grumbled. "You were lucky to be at school because time has been moving in slow motion for me with all of this going on."

"I was literally just here for Thanksgiving."

"You were only here for a few days, and we didn't want to worry you. But there's no point in trying to keep it from you any longer. Not when you're bound to notice that your father isn't at the courthouse all month. " She heaved a deep sigh. "The suspension is temporary while the judicial commission determines whether there's sufficient evidence for disciplinary action. If those bikers manufacture more evidence against him, the decision may very well go against your father. Even if they don't, he could still be removed from the bench and disbarred."

"Disbarred?" I sputtered.

"But hey, at least a grand jury hasn't been convened...yet." She lifted her glass as though she was toasting the good news. "So he might not end up in jail."

My knees felt weak, and I reached out to grab the marble counter to steady myself. "There's a chance he can go to jail? Is one of his lawyer friends representing him?"

"Absolutely not! The proceedings have been kept confidential so far, but there are already enough rumors about why your father isn't presiding over any cases. The last thing we need is for some office busybody to gossip about our business." Wrapping her fingers around my wrist, she hissed, "You can't tell anyone what's happened, Kiara. I'm doing my best to keep this situation out of the limelight while your father figures out a way out of this mess."

Appearances had always been important to my mom, so I wasn't surprised she was more worried about me blabbing than my reaction to the fact that my dad might lose his position on the bench. "You don't have to worry, Mom. I won't say a word to any of my friends. I don't want to make this any worse than it already is."

"Good." She gave me a jerky nod before lifting her glass to her lips again.

"I'm going to check on Dad," I mumbled.

There wasn't any sound coming from his office as I neared. I knocked on the door and peeked inside, my heart dropping when I saw him slumped over his desk as he ran his fingers through his hair. His head lifted, and his eyes lit up with joy when he spotted me in the doorway. "Kiara, you're home!"

"I am," I whispered, walking toward him as he got up and rounded his desk to hug me.

"I'm so happy to see you." He pressed a kiss to the top of my head. "How was your drive? I hope you didn't speed to get here early."

He sounded like his usual protective self, making my lips curve into a small smile. "Of course not, Daddy."

"Let me get a look at my girl." Gripping my shoulders, he took a step back and stared down at me. "I swear, you get prettier each time you come home for a visit. Even with the stress of finals."

"They weren't too bad," I assured him.

"I don't want you to worry, Kiara." He patted my shoulder before rounding his desk again and dropping onto his chair. "I knew when I became a judge that it could earn me some enemies."

I wasn't surprised that he was trying to downplay the situation. Odds were good that he hadn't said anything over Thanksgiving because he didn't want to cause me any distress. "Yeah, but Mom said some motorcycle club was behind all this?"

"Your mother shouldn't have bothered you with the pesky details." He shook his head with a deep sigh. "You only have a month before you go back to school. Enjoy your vacation and leave the Silver Saints to me."

"Okay." I wasn't happy as I brushed my lips against his cheek, but I knew from the determined gleam in his eyes that the subject was closed as far as he was concerned.

I didn't understand how any of this had happened, but there was one thing I knew...the Silver Saints weren't going to get away with what they'd done to my dad. For that to happen, I needed more information.

I tried to ignore the fact that my mom was still drinking wine when I walked past her on the way out to my car. Seeing her like that made me sad, so I slid into the driver's seat instead of grabbing my cell phone and heading back inside. I figured it would be difficult to find information about a motorcycle club, so I was surprised to find several news stories about the Silver Saints when I did a quick internet search. Even more shocking was that they were all positive.

Clicking through the first couple of links, I found reports on the classic car restorations that one of their guys had done and the tattoo shop they owned. None of that mattered to me—except they demonstrated that someone in the Silver Saints was good at making the club look as though they were squeaky clean—so I kept scrolling until I hit a story that mentioned the location of their clubhouse.

When I plugged the address into my maps app, I realized it wasn't that far away and decided to do a quick drive past. I didn't plan on doing anything other than getting a glimpse of their property as I pulled out of my parents' garage, but my anger against the bikers grew as I drove. By the time my phone announced that I'd reached my destination, my temper was boiling over.

Instead of doing the smart thing by not drawing attention to myself—and possibly making my dad's situation worse—I yanked the wheel to turn into their drive. The gate was closed, but a guy in a little booth jerked his head up when my tires squealed on the turn.

I threw my car into park while I waited for him to stride over to me. He was huge—tall and muscular with dark hair almost buzzed and a short-trimmed beard and mustache. My breath caught in my throat when he got close enough for me to take in his features, but not because I was intimidated—like I definitely should have been. Considering the situation, my purely feminine reaction to his piercing blue eyes was completely out of place. But that didn't stop my nipples from pebbling as his gaze raked over my face.

My mouth went dry and my dick turned to stone when I saw who was behind the wheel of the Mini Cooper.

I double blinked to make sure I wasn't dreaming. What were the odds that the woman I'd been dreaming about for a month and was planning to go after soon would show up here and unknowingly offer herself up on a silver platter?

Her eyes—which I now knew were a deep navy blue—sparked with desire, clearly shocking her, and I bit back a smile. The dark blue orbs briefly swept over my body before returning to my face. The apples of her cheeks dusted with pink, but her pretty lips mashed together, and anger swallowed her flare of interest.

I was surprised by the sudden change, but I was even more mystified at how she could look adorable and so fucking sexy at the same time.

"Lost, baby?" I grunted.

Her eyes widened just the tiniest bit at the nickname, and satisfaction rolled through me. She was obviously affected by me, which would work in my favor when I claimed her.

"No, I'm not lost!" she snapped. "I want to speak to whoever is in charge."

I raised an eyebrow at her demand. "Sure you're not lost?" She had to be. She couldn't possibly know what she was asking, and truthfully, no one spoke to a Silver Saint like that.

"You're a Silver Saint, right? A part of the motorcycle club?"

My jaw almost dropped. How did this sweet, innocent—and from the looks of her clothes and car, wealthy—little girl know anything about an MC? We weren't all that hard to find because the garage and tattoo shop were located at one end of the compound, but they had their own dedicated entrance, which still blocked them from entering the rest of the grounds. But our known location was one of the reasons we kept it heavily guarded.

"Yes! Now, I want to talk to the person in charge. I want to know why—"

"Not happening, baby," I interrupted. Her moxie was cute as fuck to me, but Mac wouldn't agree and would probably scare my curvy goddess to death. I couldn't allow that.

She gasped and unbuckled, then opened her car door. I grabbed the top to keep it from slamming into my legs or bouncing back and injuring her. But my attention was quickly stolen by her shapely legs and curvy hips as she exited the vehicle. Then she turned and leaned in to grab something. It took all my fucking energy not to grab her spectacular ass and drag her up against my body.

She stood back up and slung the long strap of a brown purse over her shoulder. Then she planted her feet and dropped her head back nearly all the way to look up at my face—trying to stare me down. I had to bite back a smile again, which should have been shocking. Being in this woman's presence made me happier than I'd been in years.

"If you won't let me drive through, then I'll just stand by the gate until it opens and find your boss by myself."

This time, I couldn't hold back a laugh. Her cheeks flamed, but impressively, she didn't look away. This girl was practically radiating sweetness and innocence, so her show of backbone made pride well up in my chest.

"How 'bout you tell me what's got you fired up, and I'll see if I can help?" I trailed off with a raised eyebrow. It was both a request for her name and a statement that I knew she was affected by me.

Her face flushed pink, and the color spread down her neck and under her shirt. *How far did it go? Was that what she'd look like when she was coming?*

"Kiara."

Her answer brought me out of my lustful haze, but the blood in my body remained in my rock-hard dick.

"Kiara," I repeated, enjoying the feel of her name on my tongue. More blood moved south, making my voice gruff when I grunted, "Knight."

"Um, okay. Knight." She licked her lips and dropped her eyes.

Fuck, the sound of my name coming from her mouth was sexy as fuck. I wanted to hear her call me by my real name, but I was afraid that if she did, I might pick her up and fuck her on the hood of her car right out here where someone could see her.

"Tell me," I demanded.

Her pretty eyes narrowed, and she planted her hands on her hips. "I want to know why you have it out for my father. What kind of people would ruin a good man? Monsters! That's what kind! What could you possibly have against him? He—"

"Hold up, baby," I interrupted her, raising my hand in the air. "Slow down. Breathe. Now, try again."

She repeated what she'd said but slower, and my brow furrowed. What the hell was she talking about?

"Who is your father, baby?"

"Jonathan Timkins," she snapped.

Fury exploded inside me at the name of that rat bastard, but then shock quickly eclipsed it. How could this beautiful girl, who smelled like flowers and blushed so innocently, be related to trash like Timkins?

Seeing her at the courthouse for the first time made more sense now.

I had always had a sort of sixth sense about people, and nothing about this girl set off any alarms. Other than the effect of her hot little body on my libido. Which had been pretty much dormant for...I couldn't remember how long.

"Who told you the Silver Saints were targeting

him, baby?" I asked curiously, trying to piece together what exactly she thought she knew.

She pinched her lips for a second, letting me know she didn't have complete faith in her source.

"My mom. But I know my dad, and he would never do the things he's being accused of!" Her beautiful eyes glistened, and something in my chest tightened. I could see that she really believed what she was saying.

Obviously, the asshole had kept her in the dark. A part of me hated to be the one to give her the truth, but I knew if it was left to any of my other brothers, they wouldn't handle her with care.

"Stay," I said quietly before spinning on my heel and entering the guard shack again. I grabbed a radio and called Grey, another patch who was splitting gate duty with me today. "Need you to start your shift early. Something came up. Got a situation to deal with."

"Need backup?" he asked through the crackle of the radio.

"Nah. Just something that can't wait."

"Be there in ten."

I stepped back outside and smirked when I saw Kiara pacing, her hands planted on her sexy hips and a scowl on her face. When she noticed me, she stopped short and growled, "Stay? I am not a dog."

Before I could stop myself, I invaded her space, pushing her back until she was up against the car and caged in when I put my hands on the roof on either side of her head. "Trust me, baby. I know you're a woman," I murmured in her ear.

She shivered, and I clenched my fists to avoid grabbing her and plastering her curves up against me. She looked so fucking soft.

"*Something* came up, huh? I can see why."

Kiara jumped at Grey's snort of amusement and began pushing on my chest to force me away. But the only thing I moved was my head when I turned to glare at my brother.

He didn't notice because he was too busy trying to get a glimpse of my girl.

"Keep it up, and we'll see how long your eyes remain in your head."

Grey's gaze snapped to mine, and he grinned at what he saw there. "I got this. Go deal with your"— his eyes dropped to where my crotch was pressed against Kiara—"situation."

Deciding to ignore him rather than deck him, I turned my attention back to the tiny goddess in my arms. "Hop in."

I reluctantly stepped back and opened her door. She stared at me with her mouth slightly open, not moving. So I gently turned her by the shoulders and gave her ass a little slap, which broke her out of her stunned state. She gasped, but before she could say anything, I ordered, "In."

I helped her down into the driver's seat, then shut her door and jogged around the hood to join her in the Mini Cooper. It was a tight squeeze for a big man like me, but it was worth it when Kiara glanced over at me and chuckled.

The pure and sweet sound washed over me, tightening something in my chest. I smiled, and her cheeks turned pink before she faced the front and squeaked, "Where are we going?"

Grey had already opened the gate, so I waved toward it, indicating that she should drive through. "Follow the drive to the right until we get to the garage by the south entrance to the compound."

It only took a few minutes to get to the side entrance to the garage. The lot in front of it was broken into spaces for bikes and others for cars or trucks. I directed her to a stall, and she carefully pulled into it, her eyes wide and round as she took in the huge trucks parked on either side of us.

"Just a short walk to my workshop. I live in the apartment above it. We'll talk there."

She halted and stared at me suspiciously. "You expect me to go with a strange man into his apartment to 'talk'?" Her fingers curled into air quotes, making me chuckle.

"Relax, baby. We can stay in the workshop. Don't worry your pretty little head. Your virtue is safe." I swallowed hard so I wouldn't add, "For now."

Kiara gasped and stared up at me in shock. "How do you know I'm a—" Her whole face flushed, and her eyes dropped to the ground.

"I didn't, baby. I was speaking metaphorically," I explained through choked laughter, amused, but also using it to disguise my primal reaction to the revelation. Knowing she would be mine and mine alone made it difficult to bury the caveman inside me.

She sputtered for a second, then seemed to just accept everything with a sigh. When her eyes met mine again, the embarrassment was gone. I felt even more drawn to this girl who could be so fierce but knew when to let things go. I hoped she used the same logic when I told her the truth about her father.

I gestured for her to walk ahead, then put my hand on the small of her back. The proprietary gesture and the scowl I shot at anyone who looked at her for more than two seconds made it clear she was with me.

Once we reached the door to my workshop, I unlocked it and turned off the alarm before ushering Kiara inside. When I flipped the lights on, Kiara looked around with awe, filling me with satisfaction. I was proud of my creations but seeing the look on Kiara's face made me feel something new.

"You're a swordsmith?" she breathed as she took in the equipment and walls filled with specialty-bladed weapons, primarily swords. "Did you make all of these?"

"Yep."

"They're amazing." She wandered to the closest one and reached up to trace some of the etchings on the blade of a saber that an Army cavalry has ordered as a gift for their retiring lieutenant.

"Feel free to look around. Be right back."

I crossed the studio to an open door that led to my office. We didn't want any of the evidence on the judge to be kept in Mac's office since he met with so many people there. So I kept it hidden away in my safe. After retrieving it, I found Kiara admiring a tiny music box with a knight in shining armor sitting on top of a horse with his sword in the air—balancing in the lid. He held a princess in his arms, and the song it played was from some movie that I couldn't remember the name of. "It's definitely not my normal kind of project," I explained when she glanced at me with a puzzled expression. "But my prez asked me to make it for his old lady, and I like a challenge."

"Well, it's beautiful," she murmured softly, her eyes a little dreamy as she looked the box over once more. I filed that away to think about later.

"Thanks. Let's sit." I pointed at a small table and chairs set by a little kitchenette. Once we were seated, I slid the files across the top, and she placed her palm on top of them. But rather than rip the first one open, she hesitated. Then her gaze raised to mine, and the fear swimming in the dark blue depths had my chest clenching again.

"I'm sorry." The softly spoken words were out of my mouth before I could stop them. I almost shook my head in exasperation. If my brothers were around to see me acting like such a pussy, I'd never hear the end of it. But the only person I was worried about was my girl.

She swallowed, then took a deep breath and put her shoulders back before opening the top folder. As she read through the files, the silence was heavy, broken only by the sounds of our breathing and her shuffling paper.

Her expression slowly went from stoic to disbelief, until it finally crumpled into devastation.

Eventually, Kiara slowly pushed the files back to the center of the table and glanced up at me. She looked so lost, I just wanted to gather her into my arms and make it all go away. But I didn't have the power to change anything. And considering the shock she had just been slapped with, I knew it wasn't the right time to force her to face the sizzling attraction building between us.

Instead, I stood and walked to her side, then held out my hand. I was about to pull my arm back when she finally grasped my palm and allowed me to help her stand. For someone so tiny, she had a hell of a grip and was squeezing the fuck out of my fingers.

My mind immediately wandered to what it would feel like if it was her virgin pussy sucking on my digits. Which only proved that I was still a bastard. She was too good for me, and I knew it. But it didn't change the outcome. I was keeping Kiara. She was mine.

However, I was resigned to letting her go—*for the moment.* "Gonna walk you to your car, baby."

She didn't say anything, and she didn't release my hand as I led her back to the parking lot.

"You gonna be okay driving?"

Kiara glanced around us, as if just realizing where we were. She dropped my hand like it had burned her and cradled her palm against her chest with the other. "Um, yes. Thank–thank you for showing me...I don't know...I can't believe...but–but..." She broke off with a little sob, and I couldn't help but lean down to kiss her forehead.

"I know you need time to let it all sink in. Give me your phone." When she didn't immediately move to comply, I grabbed her bag and dug it out myself. I quickly programmed my number in it, then hit call so I'd have hers before dropping the device back into her purse. "If you have questions or want to talk, give me a call."

Kiara sniffled for a second, then nodded before turning and climbing into her little car.

As she drove off, my gut clenched. I fucking hated that she was going back home and would be anywhere near that slimy asshole. But the fact that he'd kept her in the dark and that she'd driven into MC territory to demand answers told me that he loved his daughter. Still...I would ride out there and check on her tonight. Now that I'd found my girl again, I couldn't stay away for long.

3

KIARA

My hands shook during the drive home. I couldn't wrap my head around the evidence Knight had shown me...or my reaction to the sexy biker. If even half of the things the Silver Saints had dug up on my dad were true, he wasn't the man I thought he was. He had taught me how to ride a bicycle and blown on my scraped knees before bandaging them. Framed my artwork and put it up in his office.

How could he have also sentenced people to jail for longer terms than they deserved? And even worse, he may have helped send the innocent there, too. Defendants who hadn't broken any laws but had the bad fortune to find themselves in a crooked judge's court...my dad's.

No matter how I turned everything around in my head during the drive, it just didn't seem possible. Luckily, my mom wasn't downstairs when I got back to the house, and I was able to head straight into my dad's office without her grilling me to make sure I hadn't gone out and told the entire town about Dad's suspension. Her head would have exploded if I told her what I'd really been out doing.

So would my dad's but there was no keeping this from him. I had too many questions that needed answers, and he was the only one who could give them to me.

This time, I didn't bother knocking on the door. I just stormed into his office, stalking over to his desk and planting my hands on my hips. "It isn't all lies? You're really a dirty judge who takes bribes?"

"How can you ask me such a thing, Kiara?" He shook his head, crossing his arms over his chest. "I'm your father."

My nostrils flared as I lifted my chin. "That's a lot of blustering, but I didn't hear an actual denial."

He pushed his chair back and got to his feet with a sigh. "Because I didn't think you needed one."

"I didn't either, until I went to the Silver Saints compound and saw the evidence that they have against you." My voice wavered as tears filled my eyes. "I was so righteous when I went there, planning to confront their president. Instead, one of them showed me proof of what you did. Stuff that couldn't be doctored—actual court records."

"You don't understand." There was a deep growl of an engine outside, and Dad strode over to the window to peek through the blinds. Jumping away from the window, he turned back toward me and hissed, "Please tell me your car is in the garage."

"What in the world does that have to do with anything?"

He hurried over to me and wrapped his hand around my arm, dragging me toward the closet. "I heard the garage door open and close. If your car is in there, he won't know you're home."

My brows drew together as my gaze darted toward the window. "He who?"

"A very bad man who's not happy about my suspension since I was supposed to hear his son's case." He flung the closet door open and shoved me inside. "You need to hide. He needs to think you haven't gotten into town yet."

I didn't need him to answer my questions anymore. His reaction had already confirmed what Knight had told me.

Tears spilled down my cheeks as I dropped to the

floor and wrapped my arms around my knees, whispering, "Yes, I parked in the garage."

"Good." His eyes were pained as he stared down at me. "No matter what you hear, stay quiet and don't come out."

"What about Mom?"

"She should be fine." His gaze darted toward the ceiling. "She's passed out upstairs and won't hear a thing. He'll be long gone before she wakes up again."

I took some small comfort in the fact that my mom's heavy drinking had the unintentional benefit of keeping her safe during whatever was about to happen. I held on to that as I listened to the doorbell ring and my dad greeting the bad guy who'd come calling. "You shouldn't be here, Bickle."

"You gave me no choice, Judge Timkins," a deep voice replied. "Or should I call you Mr. Timkins now that you've been suspended?"

"I'm still a judge," my dad insisted. "The suspension is only temporary. Once I've successfully defended myself against the accusations made against me, I'll be back on the bench."

"Maybe, but that doesn't do my son much good, now does it? His case has already been assigned to another judge. One who my sources tell me isn't for sale, unlike you."

The voices came closer, and I shrank back against the wall, pressing trembling fingers against my lips to keep from making any noise.

"Your sources are correct. Thompson has earned his reputation for being a stickler," my dad confirmed.

"That's unfortunate for you," Bickle replied. "If I lose my son to prison, I'm not going to be a happy man. And like Judge Thompson, I've earned my reputation. But mine is for retribution—something you will have earned if you don't figure out a way to come through for my boy. Nobody crosses me without paying a steep price."

"There isn't much I can do while I'm suspended except give back your money."

"The cash isn't what's important, my son is. Returning my cash isn't good enough when I can't turn around and use it to bribe the other judge. So you better figure something else out, or else your daughter is going to pay the price for your incompetence," Bickle warned.

"My daughter?"

"Your little princess, Kiara." I shuddered at the malevolence in Bickle's tone as he said my name. "She should be home from college for winter break any day now, isn't that right?"

"I...uh..." my dad stuttered.

"I'm not a fool," Bickle growled. "Don't try to take me for one."

"I'm not. I swear, I'll figure something out. Just don't hurt my daughter."

"Unfortunately for you, your promises no longer mean anything to me. Which means I need to make sure I've made my point, loud and clear. And experience has proven to me the quickest way to do that is through pain." There was a loud thud, followed by my dad screaming. "Be sure to tell the doctors that you injured yourself while doing some home repairs. A hammer falling on your hand will explain away the injury."

"Yes, a hammer fell," my dad gasped in an agonized tone.

"Try to be more convincing when you're at the emergency room," Bickle chided. "Your daughter's safety depends on your ability to keep the cops out of this, after all."

My dad cleared his throat, his voice steadier as he said, "I'll do whatever it takes to keep Kiara out of this."

"Good, then we're on the same page. Two fathers looking out for their children."

I strained to listen as their footsteps headed

away. Time moved slowly while I waited for my dad to come back and tell me it was safe to come out. He was a wreck when he opened the door, his skin pale and his hair messy. "Hurry, Kiara. We have to get you out of here."

"I don't understand. Who was that guy? Where am I supposed to go?" I asked as I crawled out of the closet and got to my feet.

"All you need to know is that Bickle is someone who will not hesitate to hurt you." My dad heaved a deep sigh. "Very few people can keep you safe from him, and as much as it pains me to admit, the Silver Saints are your best bet right now."

My eyes widened. "The Silver Saints?"

"Yes, go back to their compound and ask them for protection."

"What about you?" I glanced down at the hand he was cradling against his chest. "I'm pretty sure he broke your hand."

"It's no less than I deserve for striking a bargain with the bastard in the first place, but not you. You're innocent in all this. Which is why you need to go to the Silver Saints. If Bickle can't get to you, then he can't hurt you. I can't protect you from him, but they can. Even though I almost sent one of their men to prison, from what I've heard about them, they won't turn away an innocent. Especially not a girl who needs protection from a monster like Bickle..."

His head jerked toward the window as he trailed off. "Wait, you can't leave yet. I didn't hear his truck. He might still be out there."

"Oh no." I moved toward the wall next to the window as my dad peered through the blinds again.

"Dammit, he must be waiting to see what I do or if you show up," he muttered. "Did the Silver Saints give you a way to get in touch?"

"Yes." I nodded. "I have the number for one of the guys."

"Call him. Now."

As I pulled my phone out of my pocket, I asked, "Why did you do it?"

"That's a long story best saved for another day, after I've come up with a way out of the mess that I've created so I can be certain you're safe."

His desire to protect me was what I expected from the loving father I'd grown up with, but everything else that had happened today made me feel as though I had stumbled across an alternate universe. Including the fact that I was actually looking forward to talking to Knight again...and hoping that the sexy biker would come to my rescue.

I was walking out to my bike when my phone vibrated in the pocket of my jeans. My heart skipped a beat when I saw that it was Kiara calling. I hadn't expected to hear from her so soon, and my gut was telling me that she would only be doing it if she was in danger.

"Kiara?" I answered, my voice tight with concern.

"Um, Knight?" Tears clogged her throat, and I picked up my pace until I was running to my ride. I waved a hand at Cash to get his attention. He was standing outside one of the garage bays talking to Dax, our sergeant at arms, and when I gave a signal, they jogged over to join me.

"A man came. H-He, he broke my dad's hand

and said he'd hurt me. I think he's still out there looking for me."

"You parked in the garage?" I clarified.

"Yes, and I was hiding in the closet, so he thought I hadn't come home yet. But he's not leaving." She sniffed, and her breath rattled in her lungs when she inhaled. I wanted to howl in outrage that my woman was terrified and in danger without me there to protect her.

"Stay hidden, baby. I'm coming for you." I wanted to tell her to stay on the phone with me, but my bike was gonna be loud and might hurt her ears.

"Okay," she agreed softly before the line went silent.

I cursed as I shoved my phone in my vest pocket. "My woman's in trouble," I told my brothers, ignoring their shocked expressions. Running a hand over my hair and down to hold the back of my neck, I quickly filled them in on what was happening. "You two in for backup?"

Both nodded. I was about to ask if they thought we needed more, but Dax was already on the phone with Scout. After a quick convo, he hung up and stowed his phone in his pocket. "Scout, Breaker, and Dom will be a few minutes behind us."

Without another word, Cash and Dax headed to

their bikes, then we filed out of the gate and rode to town like bats outta hell.

Considering I broke about a dozen laws to get to Kiara, it wasn't surprising that the trip took less than fifteen minutes.

As we roared up to the judge's gigantic home, a black SUV backed out of the driveway and took off.

Cash signaled to another rider, indicating that he should keep following the vehicle while the rest of us parked.

I was off my bike and sprinting to the front door the second my kickstand hit the ground. Luckily, the door was open, so I burst inside, calling Kiara's name.

In seconds, she came running down the hall toward me, tears streaming down her face. She practically leaped into my arms, and I wrapped them around her, hugging her right to me and whispering reassuring words in her ear.

The clearing of a throat stole my attention from my girl, and I looked up to see the judge had joined us in the foyer. He was cradling a bandaged hand to his chest and watching us with a deep frown.

My eyes narrowed, daring him to say one word about the way I was holding his daughter. "What the fuck is going on?" I growled. "Who is after Kiara?"

Panic entered his eyes, and he seemed to forget

all about his disapproval. "He's after me, really. But... he threatened to hurt my daughter. I...I don't know who else to turn to. She needs protection."

"After what you did, what makes you think we'd do you any favors?" The question came from Cash, who'd come in and was standing by my side. I tossed him a warning glance. There was no fucking question we would be protecting Kiara. He gave me a slight nod, letting me know he understood. Clearly, he was after something with his question.

"I know your reputation," the judge answered, his tone fearful. "You–You wouldn't turn away an innocent just because she is related to me. I—" He glanced at me speculatively for a moment, then sighed and went on. "I don't have the ability to keep her safe. I trust you to...care for and protect her."

"She can certainly trust me more than you," I growled. "That's for damn sure."

"I know. You'll...keep her safe?"

"Always," I replied firmly.

That's what Cash had been after. He wanted the judge to assure Kiara she was safe with us, and to resign himself to the fact I wouldn't be returning her. He was trying to avoid a fight when all this was over.

"Kiara? Sweetheart?" The second the judge addressed his daughter, his whole demeanor shifted.

To my surprise, his tone was gentle and eyes went soft, filling with love. It wasn't something that happened a lot, a bad guy who loved his family. You wouldn't think they would be capable, but it happened. Usually when...

I bent my head and whispered into Kiara's ear. "I need to talk to your dad, baby. Can you stay here with my brothers? That's Cash. And a few of our enforcers are guarding the door."

She reluctantly nodded and untangled herself from my hold. I passed her off to Cash—even though it almost killed me to do it. Then I glared at Judge Timkins. "We need to talk."

His expression turned wary, but he pivoted and walked to the next door on the left. When I entered his home office, I was struck by how normal it was. Everything was clearly expensive, but it wasn't over the top or in your face. It just made my theory even more plausible.

"How did you get in so deep?"

He didn't hesitate, knowing exactly what I was after. "I took money in exchange for something small and insignificant. No one got hurt from it, so I didn't think it would matter."

"It was a hook."

"Yes. Once I'd taken the first bribe, they had

leverage over me. Word got out in darker circles, and I knew I'd never be free again." He shrugged. "Except for when I was—" He cut himself off abruptly. "Anyway, I regret that Kiara got caught up in this mess." I narrowed my eyes, sure that he'd been about to reveal something, but the stubborn angle to his jaw made it clear that even if I got him to fess up, it wouldn't be easy. And I didn't have time for that shit.

"Tell me who is after you now," I demanded after he circled his desk and dropped heavily into his chair.

"I can't tell you that," he denied.

"Bullshit," I snarled, taking an intimidating pose with my feet braced apart and my arms folded over my broad chest.

"He'll kill me just for—"

"He's gonna kill you anyway if you can't give him what he wants, right?" I interrupted.

The judge winced and looked down at the desktop where his hands were clenched together. "He won't kill me. He'll go after Kiara."

"The more I know about what I'm up against, the better I can protect your daughter."

He pressed his lips together, but then his gaze strayed to a frame perched on his desk. It was a picture of Kiara. Probably a few years old because she looked younger.

She was smiling brightly, carefree and happy as she posed in what looked like some kind of dance costume. I only knew that because of the kids of my brothers who liked to dance all over the clubhouse.

Finally, he leaned back and gave me a summary of what had happened earlier. The more he told me, the angrier I got. But I forced myself to think of my girl and not how much I wanted to hunt that evil bastard down.

When he concluded, the judge turned around and pushed out of his chair. Once on his feet, he removed a painting from the wall, revealing a safe. I would have rolled my eyes at the cliché hiding spot. However, he'd chosen the best one available. It was known for being unbreakable.

After scanning his eyes and fingers, he blew into a little tube. The safe verified his identity, then he punched in a code. When the door swung open, I saw stacks of files filling it. The judge removed them and set them on the desk. Then he rummaged in a drawer for a second before producing two very large, heavy-duty rubber bands. He secured the papers on all four sides, then took a deep breath and held them out to me.

"I kept notes on everything. *Everything.* Most of them are pretty much untouchable, but this man... he's like Teflon. Nothing sticks. These are the best I can do to help protect my daughter."

Nodding, I accepted the stack and turned to leave but paused and pivoted around for one last thing. "You won't hear from Kiara or the club again until I'm satisfied that she's safe. I guarantee you'll be watched and your phones tapped."

"How will you know?"

"We'll know," I stated. "If the situation escalates or you learn anything new, go to Liquid Silver and give the information to the manager. It will get back to me."

"Jonathan!"

A shrieking voice came from the foyer, and the judge's face clouded with irritation. He stalked around the desk, and I stepped aside so he could exit, then followed.

The noise was coming from an older woman who bore a slight resemblance to my Kiara. Her face was flushed with anger, but the ruddy color of her cheeks came from consuming too much alcohol. Even the heavy makeup she was wearing couldn't fully disguise it.

"Jonathan!" she screeched again when she saw

him approach. "What are these thugs doing in my home? This one"—she pointed at Cash, who had moved to stand in front of Kiara, and her face twisted with disgust—"won't let me near our daughter!"

"Relax, Marsha," the judge sighed, barely keeping the impatience out of his tone. "I asked them to come. They are going to protect Kiara until the mess is dealt with."

"You can't be serious, Jonathan," she snapped, placing her hand on her chest dramatically. "What will people think if we just ship our daughter off to who knows where? They'll think we have something to hide! They'll think you're guilty. I won't be able to show my face at the—"

"Shut up, Marsha," he snapped harshly. "I don't give a fuck what anyone thinks as long as she's safe."

Marsha sputtered a few times. "Well, of course, I mean, obviously, Kiara is always my first priority."

The judge snorted derisively before ordering, "Go drink another bottle of wine, *dear*. I'm not sure there are any left in the cellar, but if so, I have no doubt you'll find them."

I'd heard enough of this bullshit, and I didn't want Kiara exposed to any more of it either. "Enough!" I roared, bringing an end to their bickering and garnering everyone's attention. "We're done here."

I walked over to Cash, and he immediately stepped aside so I could tuck Kiara into my side. I handed him the stack of files, then guided my woman out to my bike.

"What about my car? I didn't have the chance to bring anything into the house, so all my stuff is in the back." I glanced at his motorcycle. "And it's definitely not going to fit on there. I brought a ton since I was coming home for a month."

"A month?" Knight echoed, his brows drawing together.

"Yeah, that's what I get for winter break from school. My classes start back up the first Monday after the New Year," I explained with a nod.

I wasn't sure why, but he didn't look happy with my answer as he jerked his chin toward the group of Silver Saints sitting on their bikes at the curb in front of my parents' house. "Bickle is gonna come back when he realizes your dad can't do shit for his son.

We can't leave your car here in your dad's garage for him to find. One of the guys will disconnect the GPS and bring it to the compound. No way in hell will that bastard be able to find it—or you—there."

I darted a quick glance at his friends. "Um, why don't I just drive it myself? Everyone has their own motorcycle, and I can't imagine you want to leave one of those behind either."

He shook his head and tugged me toward his bike. "It's not gonna be a problem. Two of them will drop their bikes off, switch vehicles, and come back for your car. If you have more shit inside you want them to grab, let me know."

Thinking about all of the stuff I'd shoved into my trunk, I shook my head. "Thank you, but that's not necessary. I have everything I need already in my car."

"Good, then we can get going," he muttered, grabbing the helmet off his handlebars and handing it to me.

"Wouldn't it be easier for me to just drive it myself?" I asked again as he flung his leg over the seat and turned to hold his hand out to me.

"The only way you're leaving here is on the back of my bike, Kiara." He wrapped his fingers around my wrist and gently tugged me closer.

"Oh." My lips formed a perfect circle as I wondered why he was so insistent that I ride with him.

Stories about the meaning of having a woman on the back of your bike from romance novels that I'd read were piling together in my head. Right up until the moment he burst that bubble by saying, "Gotta keep you close so I can keep you safe."

I was happy that my dad had been right about the Silver Saints being willing to protect me in spite of what he'd done, but I hoped that Knight would have given a different reason for wanting me on the back of his bike. Like he wanted to keep me close for personal reasons...because he felt the pull between us the same as I did.

Shoving my disappointment down, I pasted on a smile and murmured, "Then I guess you better show me how to get on since I've never ridden on a motor-cycle before."

"Never?" he echoed, his lips curving into a sexy smirk.

I plopped the helmet on my head and mumbled, "Not unless you want to count the little carousel at the grocery store that I talked my dad into letting me ride once when I was three."

"Being on the back of my bike is gonna be a fuck

of a lot more fun than that, baby." He dropped his hand from my arm and pointed at a small piece of chrome with a skull imprinted on top that was sticking out toward the back of the bike. "Put your foot on the passenger peg and use my shoulder for balance. Then swing your leg back and over, just like I did."

I followed his instructions, surprised by how comfortable I felt perching on the seat behind him. "Now what?"

He reached behind me to yank me closer, and I let out a little squeal. "You gotta stick close to me while we ride, baby."

"That won't be a hardship," I mumbled under my breath.

His husky laughter let me know that I hadn't been as quiet as I thought. "Keep your feet on the pegs. They'll help you stay steady while we're riding, and they'll keep your legs away from the exhaust pipe. It gets hot as fuck, and I'd hate for you to burn your pretty legs."

"I'll be careful," I reassured him as I pressed my knees against his hips.

"I'm gonna drive fast to get you to the safety of the compound as quickly as possible, but I'll be careful too, baby. I have precious cargo on the back of my bike. No way am I going to take any unnecessary risks."

Listening to the big, muscular biker talk like that was so sweet, tears welled in my eyes. Pressing my face between his shoulder blades, I whispered, "Thank you."

"My pleasure." He twisted around and murmured, "I like that I'm gonna be your first."

I was glad the helmet hid the color in my cheeks as they heated, my imagination running away as I put a different meaning behind his words. Especially since he knew that I was a virgin.

Then he started the engine on the bike, and the rumble between my legs made me vividly aware of how damp my panties were. My entire world had fallen apart, but my mind wasn't on all of the things that had gone wrong while Knight drove me back to the Silver Saints compound. Instead, I was focused on how good it felt to be wrapped around him with the wind whipping around our bodies and his motorcycle vibrating between my legs. The last thing I should've been thinking about at the moment was sex—especially since I'd done just fine without it for nineteen years—but I couldn't stop my imagination from running wild.

Knight sparked my libido, a feat no other man

had accomplished. My body didn't seem to care about the wildly inappropriate timing. With my front pressed against his back, I was as close to him as I'd been to any man. It was a good thing I dressed warmly because my nipples were pebbled so hard that it would be impossible for Knight to miss my reaction to him without the layers between us.

By the time we pulled into the Silver Saints compound, my mind was a jumble of confusion, and my panties had gone from damp to drenched. Knight parked next to a row of three bikes in front of a large building, but when he tugged me inside, no one was hanging out in the large space with a long bar lining one side.

Knight didn't give me much time to get my bearings before he practically dragged me upstairs, down a hallway, and into a sparsely furnished room with a bed, recliner, and dresser with a television on top. "I thought you said you lived above your workshop?"

"The clubhouse is the safest place for you right now while we do some digging into the guy your dad got tangled up with." As my shoulders slumped over the idea of him dumping me in here on my own, he added, "Most of the guys keep a room here, but since my place is only a short walk away, I don't bother.

But we can use this one until we know exactly what you're up against."

Instead of leading me over to the chair, he settled me on the edge of the mattress before dropping down next to me, his deep blue eyes scanning me from head to toe. "I wasn't lying. That guy didn't hurt me. Just my dad."

"Maybe not physically, baby, but you were scared outta your fucking mind when you called me," he growled.

"That man broke my dad's hand," I whispered, tears filling my eyes again as I thought about everything I'd heard while hiding in that closet. "He really did those horrible things you said, and now he's so scared that something is going to happen to me that he practically begged me to call you for help. There's so much I don't understand. How could he betray everything he's always stood for? How could he hurt...I don't even know how many people?"

A muscle jumped in his jaw as he shook his head. "I don't know, Kiara. When we started looking into your dad, it was to make sure Rom didn't get jammed up for something he didn't do. Then when we realized it went deeper, we kept digging because we couldn't walk away knowing innocents could get hurt. We didn't turn up any motive at the time, but we weren't really looking for it. Honestly, after talking to him, I think he made some really bad decisions and ended up in so deep that he did what he had to in order to stay alive. That doesn't make it right, but it's at least an explanation."

Life was so unfair. People looked at Knight and the rest of the Silver Saints with fear, while my dad got instant respect because he was a judge. Yet they were the honorable ones. Not him. "Was he ever really the dad that I grew up with, or has he been pretending this whole time?"

Knight stroked his thumb across my cheekbone, sending a shiver of awareness down my spine. "I think he loves you. It's probably the only redeemable thing about him."

As angry as I was with my dad, I was equally in awe of Knight. "Can I ask you a question? "

"What's that, baby?"

"Why are you helping me after my dad tried to send your friend to jail for a crime he didn't commit?"

6

My gaze dropped to Kiara's pink rosebud mouth, and even though I knew the timing was shit, I couldn't stop myself from claiming it. I cupped her face in my hands and sealed our lips together. It took her by surprise, so when she gasped, I swept my tongue into her mouth.

Fuck, she tasted amazing, better than I could have ever imagined. She let out a soft whimper, and my already hard dick turned to stone. The next time she made the noise, the head of my cock leaked enough precome that I was sure I'd made a fucking mess in my jeans.

Not that I cared one fucking bit when I had heaven in front of me. Better yet...under me. Without breaking the kiss, I gently guided her back until she was lying on the bed and I hovered over her, balancing with a fist buried in the mattress on both sides of her head. After ravishing her for another few minutes, I finally released her mouth and looked into her deep blue eyes as I whispered, "That's why."

Kiara's pretty mouth formed a cute little O, tempting me to kiss her again. Instead, I rose up just enough to swing her legs up onto the bed so she was fully lying on it. Then I climbed on and covered her body with mine. She was so tiny that I eclipsed her from head to toe, and the difference in our sizes made possession well up inside until I was almost choking on it. I was more determined than ever to protect her. And to make her mine.

"I've wanted you since the moment I laid eyes on you, baby."

Her mouth curved down into a frown. "It didn't seem like it. When we met this morning—"

My laughter cut her off, and she looked at me as if I'd grown another head. "I've wanted you for so much longer than that, baby. I saw you at the court-house a little over a month ago and instantly knew you were mine. We were in the middle of all this shit with your dad, so I decided to wait until it cleared up before finding you. The other guys have had some hard-core shit go down when they found their women, and I didn't want to risk the same thing happening with you."

I closed my eyes and shook my head with another chuckle. Then I met her softened gaze and bent my head until our lips were millimeters away. "You've got no fucking idea how hard it was—and I mean that literally and figuratively—not to drag you to my apartment and sink deep inside your sweet, virgin pussy. Might have been a little gruff, but only because I was fighting to stay in control."

"Oh!" she squeaked as her cheeks bloomed with pink, and her mouth formed a shy but gorgeous smile. "You've really thought about me all this time?"

Slowly, I lowered my body until I pressed against her and my cock was nestled snugly to her center. "Thought about you. And I dreamed about what your silky skin would feel like, what your sweet pussy tasted like, and how it would feel when I was buried balls deep inside you. Woke up coming so often I bought extra sheets."

Kiara's expression of intrigue and desire was priceless. Her body knew what it wanted too because I could see her hard little nipples poking through her sweater.

Fucking hell. What I did next should have

earned me a fucking medal. "We don't know each other very well, though, so I'm willing to wait as long as it takes." I started to rise up and move off her but stopped when her legs wrapped around my waist.

Her arms wound around my neck, and she pulled my head down to whisper huskily, "I'm ready now." Come spurted from my cock at the sound of her sultry voice. She sounded so damn sexy, and her words created a crack in my resolve.

But I tried to pull away again. "You're vulnerable because of what's going on with your dad, baby. We should wait—"

"Isn't that my choice?" she asked with a quirked eyebrow.

I froze for a second, then took hold of her chin and locked our gazes so I knew she heard every word I was about to say. I wanted to make sure she completely understood.

"It is. But you better be damn fucking sure that you can handle the consequences. If I take you...once I've popped your cherry and owned your pretty little pussy...you'll be mine. There will be no going back. You'll belong to me."

I expected her to at least waver a bit, but she got a determined glint in her eyes, and her legs tightened. She nodded slowly, then murmured, "I want to be yours, Knight."

"Shane," I rasped. "You call me Shane."

"Shane?"

"My name. Knight is my road name."

"Um..." She stared at me with something akin to awe. "Isn't...isn't that a big deal? For someone to call a biker by their real name?"

I bent my head and brushed a soft kiss over her lips before answering. "It means I belong to you."

When I moved back to take in her expression, she was beaming, and her beauty took my breath away.

"Please, Shane. Make me yours."

All my resistance fled as a wave of desire filled me, and I crashed my mouth down onto hers. In the back of my mind was the knowledge that I should go slow, ease her into this, especially since she was a virgin. But fuck if I had any control over myself. I practically ripped her clothes from her body before shucking mine in record time.

When we were finally pressed together, skin to skin, relief swept through me, and I was able to grasp at a thread of sanity. "You feel so fucking good," I groaned. My mouth watered at the smell of her pussy, and my cock strained so hard it was almost painful. The bit of logic I was clinging to reminded me that I'd need to break my girl in before filling her with ten inches of my fat cock.

I pushed back and sat on my heels, my eyes roaming over my goddess. "You are gorgeous," I told her reverently. Her big tits—topped with strawberry nipples—were jiggling with her choppy breathing. Her tummy was soft, and I traced a circle around her belly button while picturing her stomach growing round with my baby. Just the thought of knocking her up had more come leaking from my dick.

Her round, full hips just added to my fantasies of Kiara carrying our babies. Her body was made for it.

Then my eyes dropped to her bare pussy, nothing hiding my view of her glistening pink lips. She was so wet that the insides of her thighs were shiny, and my mouth watered to lick it all up. And nothing was stopping me.

I knelt between her legs and pushed them as wide as they could comfortably go, then got down onto my stomach. She tried to close them, but I wedged my shoulders between her thighs to hold her open.

"Um...Shane?" I glanced up to see her watching me with trepidation, and I placed a kiss on each thigh before reassuring her. "Just trust me, baby. Let me make you feel good. I need to get this tight little pussy ready to take me."

She licked her lips and blinked, then nodded, so I went back down to focus on my treat. I inhaled deeply, taking her scent into my lungs and practically tasting it on my tongue. Using my thumbs, I parted her folds and groaned at the sight of her drenched, pink flesh. When I leaned in and licked her from bottom to top, Kiara nearly came off the bed.

"Oh, Shane!"

Grinning, I licked her like a lollipop, cleaning up her juices although it was pointless because the more I ate her, the more her cream gushed into my waiting mouth. I circled her little nub a few times, and her hips chased after my mouth when I glided back down.

"Shane," she moaned as her hands caressed my head. I captured her wrists and placed a palm on each knee.

"Hold them open for me, baby. Not done eating my dessert."

This time, I stiffened my tongue and speared her channel, grunting at the tight fit. "Fuck," I muttered against her flesh. "So damn tight. Gonna have to stretch you before I can get in there without hurting you."

She sucked in a breath, and I glanced up to see her biting her lip and watching me with worried blue orbs. "Trust me, Kiara."

After a second, she whispered. "I do."

As a reward, I attacked her pussy with gusto, finally sucking on her bundle of nerves and pushing her over the edge.

"Shane! Oh! Oh! Yes! Yes!" Her whole body shook from the onslaught of pleasure. While she was in the throes, I sucked on her clit and pushed a single finger inside her channel. I moved it around, stretching her and rubbing the spot inside that catapulted her right into another orgasm. That allowed me to get another finger inside. By the time I'd managed to squeeze four digits in there, I'd lost count of how many times she'd climaxed.

"I can't...I can't..." she mumbled as she flopped back on the mattress like a limp noodle.

I smiled and crawled up and over her until the head of my cock kissed her entrance. "You will," I argued firmly.

"But—oh! Ooooooh!" She moaned as I slowly pushed in. I'd barely gotten inside when her pussy clamped down, and I exploded.

"Fuck!" I shouted. I'd come way too fucking early. Or at least...I thought I did. Except I was still as hard as a rock. This brought a little smirk to my lips. The more times I came inside her, the more likely I was to knock her up. The thought brought me up short.

"Kiara, are you on anything?"

"W–W–What?" She was barely coherent, but I needed to know.

"Baby, focus. Are you on birth control?"

"No, I–oh, yes! Shane!"

I pressed my thumb firmly over her clit, spiraling her into another climax. Knowing it would hurt no matter what I did, I used her orgasm to distract her as I got it over with in one thrust. Bucking my hips hard, I tore through her barrier and glided into heaven until I was sheathed from root to tip.

Tears leaked from Kiara's eyes, and I quickly swept them away and kissed each wet spot. "I'm so sorry, baby. I promise it will only hurt like that once. You okay?"

She sniffed and nodded. "I think so." Then she shifted, and I grabbed her hips.

"You gotta stay still, baby, or I won't be able to hold back."

To my astonishment, she rose up and kissed me

with fervor as her legs curled around me once more, sliding me impossibly deeper so that my cock butted up to her cervix.

"Mmm," she hummed softly. The sound sent whatever blood was left in my brain rushing straight to my cock.

Keeping my grip on her hips, I elevated her pussy and retreated nice and slow before slamming in with so much force the headboard knocked into the wall.

"Fuck!"

"Yes!"

We both cried out at the same time, and it released the animal inside me, filling me with a primal need to satisfy my woman and breed her.

I kept the rhythm of out slow and in fast, but eventually, I was rutting between her thighs in a frenzy. My hands glided up to cup her tits, and my thumbs brushed over her nipples as I massaged the generous globes.

"Oh, Shane! Harder! Yes! That's it! Oh, yes!"

"Love how fucking loud you are, baby," I growled as I pinched the stiff buds. "Let me hear it. I want to hear what I do to you."

I changed my angle, and she yelled at the top of her lungs, "Right there! Yes! Yes! Yes!" Her hips pumped up to meet me as I practically pounded her into the mattress.

"Come, baby. Squeeze that tight pussy and milk all of the come from my cock. Oh, fuck yeah. Doing so good, baby. Oh, fuck!"

Kiara's body began to shake, and her muscles clenched, signs that she was about to reach the peak. Suddenly, she froze and panted, "You have to pull out. I'm not on anything, Sh—"

"Not a fucking chance," I growled as I grabbed her hips again, angling them up so she would take everything I gave her and suck it deep into her unprotected womb. "Gonna blow inside you, baby. Paint the walls of your pussy with my spunk. Now be a good little girl and come so your cervix is nice and soft when I fill you with my seed."

I pulled out and brought one of my hands down on her pussy before stuffing her full again. Kiara's head flew back, and her back bowed as she screamed so loud it made my ears ring. The feel of her pulsing muscles contracting around me, sucking me impossibly deeper, set me off right along with her.

Jets of come spurted from my dick, filling her so full that it leaked out between us. My orgasm felt like it was never ending, but eventually, I seemed to be drained.

But when I moved to withdraw from her heat, I was still mostly hard.

Kiara mewled in protest, and her thighs tightened. "Don't leave me yet," she whispered.

I placed a soft kiss on each puckered nipple, then a lingering one on her lips. "Never, baby."

She sighed, and just like that, I was once again sporting a steel rod between my legs and more than ready to fill her with another round of baby batter. But she needed to rest, so I flipped us over, sprawling her body on top of mine so I stayed snug inside her.

My good intentions went out the window when she sat up to say something. Instead, her face took on a look of ecstasy. She rode me hard before collapsing on my chest and falling asleep.

Although I tried to let her rest, I lost the battle a couple of times, waking up starving and knowing her pussy was the only thing that would satisfy my hunger.

Not that she seemed to mind.

W hen I woke up the following morning, my body ached in places I didn't know were possible. I was surprised to find that I enjoyed them because each twinge reminded me of what I'd done with Shane last night, and I didn't regret any of it. Not even allowing him to come inside me so many times without a condom.

Losing my virginity to him hadn't been anything like what I'd expected...the experience had been a thousand times better than I ever could've imagined. He'd taken such good care of me—before, during, and after we'd had sex.

His arms tightened around me, and the bristles of his beard scraped my skin as he buried his face in my neck and murmured, "Morning, baby. Get enough sleep?"

I twisted in his embrace to grin up at him. "Barely."

My stomach fluttered as his lips curved into a smile of pure male satisfaction. "Can't blame me for needing more of your sweetness, baby."

Remembering exactly how he'd woken me up each time—with his mouth between my legs—my cheeks heated. I ducked my head, pressing my cheek against his broad chest as I mumbled, "I don't."

"Stop that, baby." He pressed his finger against my chin to tilt my head back, brushing his lips against mine. "You don't have anything to be embarrassed about. You giving yourself to me last night was the best damn thing that's ever happened to me."

This time, it was my heart that fluttered. "Didn't you get the memo that bikers aren't supposed to be sweet?"

"When it comes to our women, the Silver Saints are sweet as fuck." His laugh was rueful. "I gave the guys so much shit for it, but now that I found you, I finally realized I'm no different."

I loved how he called me his, but I didn't want to read too much into it. Guys said all kinds of things to get women to sleep with them. Not that I knew from experience or anything.

My cheeks heated even more, but I was saved from any questions about it because Shane's cell phone rang. He rolled over and reached out to grab it from the pocket of his jeans on the floor. "Shit, it's my prez. Sorry, baby, I gotta take this."

I stroked my hand up his back with a nod. "It's okay. He might have news about that Bickle guy."

"Hey, Mac." There was a brief pause before he turned to look at me. "Sure, I'll bring her down in a minute."

I waited until he disconnected the call to ask, "Was I right? Did he have news?"

He shook his head. "Not yet, but he wants to meet you."

"Oh." My lips formed a perfect circle as my eyes widened.

"Don't worry, baby. You're always gonna be safe with me, and my MC brothers will have your back just like they do mine."

My father's betrayal was fresh in my mind—and heart—but I somehow knew deep down inside that I could trust Shane. Even though I'd only known him for one day, he'd gone out of his way to make sure I was safe when he didn't have to. His selflessness had proven to me that he was a stand-up guy. Unlike my dad.

Scrambling to my knees, I nodded. "I'm a little nervous, but I know you won't let anything happen to me."

"Damn straight," he grunted.

After we got dressed and ready to head downstairs, he threaded his fingers through mine to lead me to the Silver Saint president's office. Mac was as intimidating as I'd expected him to be...until two women walked in behind us, and his gaze landed on one of them. His expression immediately softened, and it was impossible to miss the love in his eyes.

"What did you need, baby?" he asked as Shane got me settled in a chair in front of his desk before shoving the other closer to me and dropping onto it.

"Sorry, I didn't mean to interrupt." Her gaze darted toward me, and she offered a sweet smile. "Erin and I were going to make some breakfast, and I wanted to know if you wanted three or four eggs."

He quirked a brow. "You gonna do your specialty?"

"Of course," she huffed.

"Gimme four then." He beckoned her closer with his index finger. "But I need a kiss first."

"You always do." She giggled and shook her head as she padded over to brush her lips against his.

I was happy to discover that Shane hadn't been kidding about the Silver Saints being sweet when it came to their women. It boded well for me if we ended up together for real, after everything was settled with my dad.

The other woman came close and introduced herself. "I'm Erin."

"Nice to meet you. I'm Kiara."

Her gaze darted between Shane and me, a knowing gleam in her eyes that made me blush. "Would you like to join us for breakfast?"

"Um..." I looked at Mac. "I could eat, but I'm not sure what I have going on this morning."

He smiled at me. "Your schedule is wide open as far as I'm concerned. I just wanted to meet you and let you know that you have the full support and protection of the Silver Saints behind you."

"Thank you," I whispered. "Shane told me the same."

Mac chuckled. "I'm sure he did."

"Great," the other woman chirped. "Now that all that's settled, you can join us in the kitchen while we make breakfast then."

"Do me a solid and don't grill my woman too hard, Bridget," Shane growled.

"Who me?" She flashed him an innocent smile. "I guess I can leave it to all the guys who pop in to see what we're cooking instead."

"Shit," Shane muttered, getting up to pull me to my feet as he shrugged out of his leather vest. Settling it over my shoulders, he pulled my arms through the holes. "Wear this for me, baby."

My brows drew together as I nodded. "Um, okay."

"Good call," Mac murmured.

Bridget and Erin chuckled while they led me out of the office. As we headed down the hallway, I warned, "I'm not sure how much help I'll be unless you want to do little signs for each dish or place setting. I'm a horrible cook, but I'm a heck of a calligrapher and can draw."

Erin glanced at me over her shoulder. "Really?"

I nodded. "Yeah, I'm an art major."

"I bet you'll get along great with my husband. He's a tattoo artist."

"Nice!" I'm not sure why, but I lifted my arm to show my bare skin. "I don't have any ink, but I really respect anyone who can take their art and put it on someone's body. That has to be a huge compliment, that people want to wear your art for the rest of their lives."

"Do you have any of your drawings with you?" Erin asked. "I'd love to see them sometime."

"I had my current sketchbook in my car, so it should be upstairs in the room Shane and I were… um…using last night." My cheeks heated as I added, "Someone brought my suitcase up for me so I'd have my clothes and toiletries."

"I'll take you up to grab it," Bridget offered.

"Oh, I'm sure I can find the room myself."

She hooked her arm through mine. "Trust me, Knight doesn't really want you wandering around by yourself even though you're wearing his cut."

"Yeah, it's a little weird that he put it on me," I murmured as we headed upstairs. "I thought these vests were sacred to bikers."

"Oh, sweetie. They are," she confirmed with a smile. "But their women are even more so."

"Wow," I breathed, my mind spinning over the implication of what she'd said. My heart raced over the possibility that Shane really meant it when he called me his. I'd been starting to wonder if all his talk about me belonging to him might have been in the heat of the moment. Maybe…well, I hoped he'd meant it. Especially since we'd taken so many risks by not using protection.

My head was in the clouds as I dug through my suitcase to grab my sketchbook and pencils before heading back to the kitchen. While Erin and Bridget started making breakfast, I flipped through my drawings to the one I'd been working on between studying for finals. Erin wandered over while I was sketching and gasped. "Wow, you weren't kidding about being good."

Her compliment meant a lot since my art was my passion. "Thanks."

"Can I see more?"

"Sure." I turned my sketchbook toward her and let her flip through the pages. When she got to one with a mermaid coming out of the waves during a storm, she paused and leaned closer. "Okay, you really need to talk to Patriot. He's been stuck on a design for one of his regular customers because he can't quite get the mermaid right. I bet you could help him figure it out."

"Oh, I couldn't possibly." I shook my head. "I've never done something like that before."

She tapped her finger against the drawing. "Trust me, your skills are more than up to the task."

"Do you really think so?"

Bridget came over to look at my sketch. "Definitely. You guys should go talk to him now. I can take care of breakfast."

Erin didn't hesitate to take her up on the offer. She snatched my pad off the table and wrapped her fingers around my wrist to tug me to my feet. "C'mon, don't be shy. I've been dealing with a grumpy husband for way too long, and you're my ticket to being the one who gets to solve his problem for him when it's usually the other way around."

"Well, I guess when you put it that way, I'd love to help." Especially when I owed the Silver Saints for keeping me safe after what my dad tried to do to one of them.

"She fits you," Mac said gruffly as he stroked his beard and stared at the door our women had disappeared through.

"Yeah, she does," I agreed with a grin. "How soon do you think we could get her a vest?"

Mac grabbed his cell and hit a button, then waited. When the other person picked up, he grunted, "Scout, stop by Rider's office and have him check our inventory of property vests on your way here." He listened, then grunted again and hung up.

"Thanks."

Mac nodded. "Cash dropped off the files last night. Only managed to get through a small chunk. Scout rounded up a few brothers to help us get through them faster. I want to know who this asshole is. I understand that your first priority is protecting your woman—"

"Damn fucking straight," I growled.

Mac tossed a look that clearly said to shut the fuck up. "Like I was saying, I understand that your first priority is protecting your woman—as it should be. But we aren't going to stop with just her. This guy clearly needs to be taken down and his operation dismantled. Just from what I've learned so far, he's got his fingers in everything from human trafficking to drugs to weapons. I'd be willing to bet my cut that he makes a habit of finding weak people in the right places that he can exploit and keep them doing his bidding through blackmail and intimidation."

The next two hours proved him right. Timkins hadn't managed to break all of the coded information, so our knowledge had holes. Still, we had a lot to go on. Hack took the files to run through a program he'd built that would organize and catalog them into a database for us to use, particularly for his web crawlers.

"Cash, take Doc and go nose around, see if there is any chatter about what might happen with Bickle's kid when Timkins doesn't come through for them. If there is a jailbreak, or whatever, planned, I want to know about it." Cash nodded at Mac and left.

"I called a couple of our informants from some of the...less than upstanding clubs nearby," Scout announced. "Grey's gonna take a handful of prospects and send them on meets with them while he does his thing with the computers in the van."

Mac handed out some other assignments before finally looking at me. "I'll keep you updated. For now, go take care of your woman. Better get her used to MC life since it's her future. Besides, I know you're slammed with Christmas orders."

I wanted to argue, to tell him to give me something that would help move this along and ensure Kiara's safety. But he wasn't wrong on either count. I was a little backed up at the studio, and ensuring Kiara understood an old lady's life and fit in here was important to keeping her.

That made me wonder how things were going with Bridget and Erin. I hadn't intended to be away from her for so long. I hoped that since we hadn't been disturbed—other than Bridget dropping off Mac's breakfast and a plate for me—it meant Kiara had hit it off with the girls.

When I exited Mac's office, I made a beeline for the kitchen. I was anxious to see my girl, and I doubted I'd last more than a few minutes before I was dragging her sexy ass back to bed. Just thinking about her delicious curves had my groin tightening.

Since breakfast was long over, I didn't expect to find Kiara still in the kitchen but decided to check there first. As I'd suspected, they were no longer there, but none of the current occupants had any idea where they'd gone. They weren't in the lounge or the activity room, or the kids play area. Figuring she might have lain down for a nap—she hadn't had a lot of sleep the night before—I took the stairs two at a time to the room we were staying in. When she wasn't there either, my mood plummeted. Where the fuck was she? I knew Erin and Bridget wouldn't let her wander alone even though she was wearing my vest, so they had to be together. But no one seemed to know where that was. Until I checked the garage and found Rylee, Nova's old lady and a talented mechanic, rolling out from underneath a car.

"Have you seen Bridget or Erin?" I asked impatiently.

Rylee grinned as she wiped her hands on a cloth. "Are you asking about those two or the knockout blonde with them?"

I mentally snapped at her for not just answering my damn question and trying my patience, but if

Nova lurked anywhere near, he'd break my jaw if I did it out loud.

"Any of the three," I grunted.

She laughed and pointed at a door that led from the garage bays to the back office of Silver Ink. "Nova mentioned that your lady is quite the talented artist. Apparently, Patriot has taken an interest in her."

I hadn't been aware that Kiara was an artist, and I felt a wave of fury that someone else was appreciating her talents before me. I was even angrier with myself for not knowing every single thing there was to know about my woman. This wasn't rational, considering the time we'd been together, but nothing about Kiara and me was rational.

I was also aware that Rylee was purposely egging me on, but fuck me if I could keep from letting it get under my skin.

Nova ran Silver Ink, and he and Patriot were the best tattoo artists in the business. If they thought Kiara was talented, that was huge, but I'd have to learn to be happy for her about that another time. Right at that moment, I was too busy trying to fight the urge to kill one or both of my brothers. Each one was as gone over their old ladies as I was over Kiara, but that logic wasn't having much luck penetrating my jealousy.

"Thanks," I grunted as I stomped over to the door. It slammed against the wall when I yanked it open and marched through the back and out onto the main floor, where several stalls had the equipment needed to ink someone's skin. The last stall was bigger and held a large design table and walls with corkboards for ideas and partial or finished sketches.

Kiara sat at the table, bent over a pad with her hand moving a pencil quickly over the page. Bridget and Erin sat across from her, looking like proud mama hens. Patriot was seated around the corner of the table, close enough to be able to watch carefully but far enough away to be respectful of her space and her old man. I had to admit, albeit begrudgingly, that I had no reason to pick a fight with him.

Irritated, I walked up behind Kiara, interrupting her flow when my shadow fell over her sketch pad. She glanced up with a frown, but when she saw me, her entire face lit up, and her irritation dissolved into a beautiful smile.

"Hi!" she chirped as she swiveled her stool around and rose just enough to kiss my cheek.

"That is not how you greet your man, baby," I

muttered right before I took her mouth in a deep kiss that left her breathless and in a daze of passion.

Smirking, I turned her around and tucked her into my side before leaning forward to examine her drawing. "Wow."

My exclamation seemed to shake off the fog, and excitement infused her expression. "Do you like it?"

"It's beautiful, baby. I had no idea you were an artist."

"Well"—she shrugged—"we haven't known each other long. I'm sure we'll learn everything there is to know about each other soon enough."

"We can check what you sound like when you come, what your sweet pussy tastes like, and how fucking gorgeous you look spread beneath me with my cock buried inside you off the list," I whispered in her ear, making her blush hard.

"She helped me with a design I've been stuck on for weeks," Patriot informed me, clearly impressed. "When I asked her about the design for another client coming in next week, she drew this."

The drawing depicted an intricate gemstone tattoo that looked sort of like a shoulder epaulet. It started with a large jewel on the top of the shoulder, then layers of beaded strings swagged over the shoulder and down the arm, all dripping with jewels.

About halfway down was another large stone in a setting that made it look like an antique brooch, then a few more swags of beads and jewels until the design ended at the elbow. Even in a black-and-white sketch, the jewels looked as if they were sparkling on the skin. I could only imagine what it would look like in color.

"Incredible," I praised, giving her a light squeeze.

Patriot reached for the drawing, and I quickly snatched it from his grasp. "Mine," I growled. Then I lifted Kiara off the stool and took her hand, guiding her out of the shop and taking her back to my studio. I couldn't help grumbling about her using her art to help Patriot instead of me. Apparently, I wasn't quiet enough about it because Kiara burst out laughing.

When we entered the studio, I guided her around the work tables and large machines until we reached the same area where I'd first shown her the proof of her father's dirty dealings. I hoped to make happier memories here so she would want to be with me while I worked.

"I think it's super sweet that you want me all to yourself, Shane," she giggled. "But I doubt you make things like this." She pointed at the bejeweled drawing.

"Is that so?" She raised an eyebrow at my smug tone.

I walked to a cabinet where I stored finished pieces and retrieved an oblong box before returning to the table. I opened the lid to reveal a dagger, and Kiara gasped in awe. "You made this?"

I nodded, practically preening under her approval...like a jackass.

"The pommel, handle, and crossguard are antique silver-plated cast metal." A detailed swirling design engraved in the metal incorporated rubies and sapphires into many of the curls. "The blade is spring steel since this is a medieval reproduction." On it were elaborate, black-colored medieval designs engraved from the hilt down to the central ridge.

"It's breathtaking," she whispered as she took the dagger and studied it from different angles. I noticed she was careful not to touch the blade, impressing me even further. When bare fingers touch the blade, some of the natural grease/oil of the skin is left on it. This grease was slightly acidic and would corrode it if left uncleaned. Just one night uncleaned would leave a corroded fingerprint on a sword or dagger.

"I took an art history class that spent some time on weaponry," she admitted with a soft laugh.

I grinned and leaned back in my chair, crossing

my arms over my chest. "You couldn't be more perfect for me if you tried."

Kiara's cheeks flamed with pink, but she smiled back at me with sparkling blue eyes. I loved seeing her so happy, especially after the devastation she'd been hit with the day before.

"I have a client who wants a set of Katana swords for his father. Would you like to help me with the design?"

Kiara jumped up and clapped her hands excitedly, then plopped back down in her seat with skin flushed from the roots of her hair down to where it disappeared beneath her sweater.

"You're cute as fuck," I told her with a chuckle. Then my smile turned devilish. "But you're also hot as sin." I swept her into my arms and stalked across my office to the staircase, jogging up to my apartment. We'd sleep at the clubhouse for her safety, but first, I was gonna worship her sexy curves in our bed.

9

KIARA

Settling into life in an MC compound turned out to be much easier than I ever could have expected. Everyone had been so accepting of me, even Rom. In some ways—like never having to cook because someone else always took care of it—things were even similar to my parents' house. And in others, it was wildly different. Especially my nights spent in Shane's bed.

A few days after he'd come to get me, he felt as though it was safe enough to stay in his apartment instead of the room in the clubhouse we'd been using. We'd visited it a few times, but I didn't see much more than the bed back then.

For the past week and a half, we'd been mostly in a private bubble between his workshop and bedroom, except when we headed back to the club-house for meals. Although that only started up a week ago since food had miraculously appeared on his doorstep for several days.

It turned out that bikers weren't just sweet with their women. They also liked to matchmake for their friends. Not that Shane really needed any help in that area since I'd already fallen hard for him. How could I not when he was so darn attentive and had no problem telling and showing how much he wanted me?

Lifting his welding helmet off and setting it on the steel workbench, he tugged off his thick gloves and stalked across the room toward me. He'd set up a space for me to draw as far away from where he did his forging as he could make it so that I'd be safe from any sparks.

Setting my sketchbook next to me and tilting my head back to stare up at him, I asked, "All done?"

"As close as I'm gonna get for now."

I tapped my pencil against the pad before setting it on top. "You don't need to rush on my account. I can keep myself busy for as long as you need. You know how I lose track of time while I'm drawing."

"Lasted as long as I'm gonna," he muttered. "Missed out on my favorite way to start the day, and now I can't wait another minute to fill my mouth with your taste."

He was super close to the date he was supposed to ship the sword he was working on, so today I'd snuck out of bed and headed down to the workshop before he woke up. He was only about fifteen minutes behind me, but I'd texted Erin to ask her to bring over breakfast—I wasn't supposed to leave the building unless I was with Shane or another Silver Saint—and she showed up while he was kissing the heck out of me.

After we ate, I insisted that he get some work done before we did anything else. Shane hadn't been happy about it, but he'd reluctantly agreed when I'd fake pouted and told him that I was excited about a drawing I was working on for the medieval sword and scabbard he was going to make next.

I twined my arms around his neck as he lifted me out of my seat. "Are you sure you got enough done? I don't want to be responsible for messing up your business because you disappointed a customer and they post a scathing review online."

"So fucking sweet." He brushed his lips against mine before heading into his office and crossing toward the stairs. "But you don't need to worry, baby. This dude has ordered from me before and would wait as long as he had to for one of my pieces because I'm the best."

I grinned up at him. "And so humble."

"I'm not gonna pretend I don't have skills when I damn well know I do."

His confidence was so sexy. "Lucky for me, you save the best of them for the bedroom."

"And you're about to experience them up close and personal until you're screaming my name over and over again."

"Yes, please," I breathed, pressing my thighs together to ease the ache his words had caused in my core.

When we got to the apartment, he stopped in the living room to set me on my feet before hooking an arm under my leg to lift it to his hip. I let out a little squeak of surprise and held on tight. I was wearing a pair of leggings, and he slid his hand under the waist and into my panties to palm my bare butt cheek. "I hate to admit it, but you found the best way to motivate me to get shit done. I don't think I've ever been that productive in such a short amount of time."

"I think you deserve a reward for being such a hard worker."

"I know exactly what I want." His hand dipped lower to cup my core. "And judging by how drenched you are for me, you want my mouth on you just as much as I do."

"Yes," I panted as he glided his fingers through my wetness.

Lowering my leg, he dropped to his knees and tugged my leggings and panties down until I could kick them off. Then he wasted no time devouring me. Propping one of my legs over his shoulder, he licked between my pussy lips from bottom to top before circling my sensitive bundle of nerves. I clenched his shoulders with a moan, and he continued to lap at me.

My legs shook each time he sucked my clit into his mouth, and it didn't take long until I felt as though I was about to fly apart. "I'm so close."

"Come for me, baby." He turned his head to nip at my inner thigh. "Want your taste to fill my mouth when I sink my cock into your tight pussy."

He went back at me with his mouth as he sank a finger into my channel, and fireworks exploded behind my eyes. He ate me through my release, and as soon as the shudders subsided, he jumped to his feet, swept me off mine, and wrapped my legs around his waist to carry me into the bedroom. "I'll never get enough of you coming all over my face."

He stalked over to the bed and tossed me onto

the mattress, making quick work of stripping out of his clothes. "Or feeling your pussy wrapped around me, milking my come from my cock until it's dripping down your thighs."

I ate up his naked body with my gaze and stretched my arms out to him. "Then don't wait."

"So fucking perfect," he murmured, crawling until he was hovering over me with his palms pressed into the mattress on both sides of my body. "Not sure what the fuck I ever did to get so lucky, but I'll be grateful for it every damn day of my life."

"You're pretty darn perfect yourself, especially when you say sweet things like that." I brushed my fingers over the scar on his shoulder before twining my arms around his neck and pulling him close for a kiss.

When he lifted his head, we were both breathless, and he had the tip of his dick notched at my entrance. "That's because we're perfect for each other, baby."

I was so wet from the orgasm he'd given me that he easily pushed inside me with one powerful thrust. He was so big that he stretched me past the point of comfort, but I had quickly grown to appreciate the sensation. Just something about being filled by him made me feel...whole. I knew it sounded corny, but no other word explained it as well.

"Shane," I gasped.

Shoving my shirt up, he flicked open the front clasp of my bra to cup one of my breasts. My inner walls fluttered when his thumb swept across my pebbled nipple. "Your pretty tits are so damn sensitive. I bet I could make you come just by playing with them."

He lowered his head and swirled his tongue around the other nipple before sucking it deep into his mouth. Then he let the puckered peak go with a pop. "But not today. No way in hell can I pull my cock out of your sweet heat to find out. You feel too damn good."

Shifting his hips back, he dragged his hard length against my inner walls before he slammed back inside. "Oh my gosh. Yes!"

"You gonna give me what I want, baby?" he grunted, picking up the pace. "Let me fuck you until you're screaming my name, your pussy walls gripping me so tight that I can't do anything but lose control?"

"Yes," I panted, digging my nails into his shoulders as I held on for the wild ride.

"Damn straight," he growled, wedging his arm

between our bodies to circle my clit. "'Cause you're mine."

I wrapped my legs around his waist, my breasts bouncing with each of his brutal thrusts. "Yours."

"I'm the only man who's ever gotten to taste you." He captured my mouth for a deep kiss. "The only one who knows what it feels like to have your pussy wrapped around his cock." He swiveled his hips, bringing me closer to the edge. "And damn well the only one whose come has dripped down your thighs. I'll be the last, too. But I can't hold on much longer, baby. Give it to me. Let me feel you milk every ounce of my seed from my cock with your sweet pussy."

His dirty, possessive words were all it took to send waves of pleasure crashing over my body. My cries echoed against the walls, intermingling with his roar of completion. When the shuddering finally ended, I collapsed against the mattress in an exhausted heap. I'd only been awake for a few hours, but I couldn't keep my eyes open. I'd never been a person who napped, but I was so exhausted that I drifted off to sleep while Shane padded into the bathroom to get a washcloth. I didn't even wake when he cleaned me up.

My phone beeped, and I leaned back so I could stretch out my arm to grab it without disturbing Kiara. She'd been exhausted lately, so I wanted her to sleep as long as she could.

Mac: Doc convinced Timkins to contact Bickle. Got us a meet. Be ready to ride in an hour.

I sent back a confirmation, then put down my phone and curled back around my woman. Leaving her soft, naked body in this warm bed without me was not how I wanted to start my day. But I was relieved that we were finally making progress with the threat against my girl.

Reluctantly, I whispered a kiss across her temple,

then gingerly scooted away before sitting up and swinging my legs over the side of the bed. Picking up my phone so it wouldn't wake her if one of my brothers called or texted, I carried the device into the bathroom and set it on the sink.

After gathering up fresh clothes, I hopped into the shower. I was almost done when the door banged open, and Kiara came bolting into the bathroom. She dropped to her knees in front of the toilet, and I jumped out of the shower, making it to her just in time to hold her hair back. She emptied her stomach, then dry heaved a few times before collapsing back into my arms.

"You okay?" I murmured.

"Other than feeling like total crap. Sure, I'm fine."

I chuckled, glad she was feeling human enough to be sarcastic. Carefully, I helped her to her feet and over to the sink. She rinsed her mouth, then took the toothbrush I held out and quickly brushed her teeth.

"Maybe I have the flu?" she wondered. I scooped her into my arms and carried her back to bed. "Except I don't always feel this sick. Tired, sure... but..." She trailed off on a yawn, and when I gently laid her down, she almost immediately drifted off to sleep again. This was the third morning in a row that

Kiara had woken up and ran straight to the bathroom to vomit.

I had a feeling I knew the cause, but even if I was willing to wake her, we didn't have time to get into it before I had to meet Mac. And Bickle wasn't the type of guy who rescheduled.

A glance at the clock on the bedside table lit a fire under my ass, and I swiftly dressed and grabbed my gear, keys, and wallet.

I left Kiara a note on her nightstand, telling her I was running an errand and would be back soon. Also, ordering her to rest and that I would have someone come by with food for her.

Then I headed out to meet my brothers and go for a ride.

MAC, Cash, Rom, Breaker, and Dom all strutted into a large warehouse where we were met by a tall man in a black suit, as well as half a dozen other well-dressed males. We'd left our additional backup outside, but I had no doubt these guys were aware of the eight armed bikers waiting for a signal from us.

"Gentlemen."

Dom snorted at the greeting. "Not a word I'd use to describe us, but if it makes you feel better..."

Mac cuffed Dom on the shoulder and shot him a look. Normally, he would step forward and take the lead in situations like this, but Mac was a firm believer in handling your own shit with the support of your family. Seeing as how this situation revolved around my girl, he remained with the others as I walked up to the slimy son of a bitch who'd threatened Kiara.

"Bickle?" I clarified.

The man in the black suit nodded. He looked calm and collected, the epitome of confidence. But the guarded look in his eyes confirmed our plan would work.

"You know who we are?" I asked in a low, dangerous tone.

"Silver Saints, I presume?"

"Right. So you know we don't fuck around. Especially when a situation involves one of our own."

Bickle's composure cracked for just a second, showing confusion and wariness. "Timkins isn't one of your own. He nearly destroyed the life of one of your brothers. Shouldn't you be paying him a visit, rather than wasting my time?" If I weren't watching him so closely, I might not have seen the signs that he was blustering.

"Depends on which Timkins you're referring to, Bickle." I reached out behind me and caught the vest I knew Rom would toss to me. I held it up and displayed first the front, which had Kiara stitched over one breast. Then I flipped it around so he could see the big-ass property patch on the back.

"His daughter is yours?" Fear was bleeding into Bickle's tone.

"She is."

He swallowed hard but squared his shoulders to try to keep up his tough-guy charade.

"I was unaware of her ties to the Silver Saints. She won't have anything to fear from me going forward."

"What the fuck?" Another greasy snake in an expensive gray suit stepped up to Bickle's side. "You're not going to take out revenge for my brother's death sentence because the bitch is fucking this asshole?"

Before the guy could say another word, a loud pop sounded, and he dropped to the ground, holding the gushing wound on his thigh—less than two inches from the family jewels—and screaming in agony. I lowered my arm but didn't relax my grip on my gun. "You should really put a muzzle on your mutt," I growled.

All of Bickle's men had whipped out their own weapons, pointing them at us. I doubted even one of my brothers had bothered to reach for their gun. That was the difference between the two crews in the warehouse. The Silver Saints didn't need to brandish our weapons to put the fear of God into whoever we were facing off with. We'd use 'em—and there wasn't one of us who wasn't an expert marksman—but only if there was no other choice.

These idiots were using their guns to intimidate, but even if they were stupid enough to think we'd cower, Bickle wasn't.

"Put them away," he snapped. "You shoot one of them, and you'll bring down the entire fucking MC on our heads."

Maybe he was smarter than I thought.

"I apologize for my son's outburst. Now, as I said, your woman no longer has anything to fear from me. Are you finished?"

"When I said Timkins, I was referring to the family," I replied. "It'll be hard enough for my woman to watch the father she thought she knew facing what he's done in court. I don't want her to be grieving his death."

"You can't be serious," Bickle sputtered. "You're extending your protection to the judge?"

I nodded. "And her mom."

Bickle was silent for an extended period. But eventually he waved a hand and muttered, "Fine. Fine. We won't harm your woman or her parents."

Something in his eyes when he agreed was off, but I wasn't sure what it was. I had no doubt he wouldn't harm the Timkins, yet I felt uneasy.

I glanced at Mac and saw him watching Bickle with the same suspicious expression. Then he stepped up to say one last thing. "Silver Saints have a rep for protection. But don't forget that we also have one for being ruthless motherfuckers. You break the deal we just struck, and before I let Knight kill you, I'll make sure you wished you were never born."

The little shit crying on the floor glared at me, and I was feeling petty, so I took another shot at the pavement in front of his face. "I'll be waiting for you to give me a reason."

———

WHEN I RETURNED to the compound, Breaker waved me over after we'd parked our bikes. He typed something on his phone, then said, "Your old lady is with mine in the kids' playroom."

"Thanks," I said as I slapped him on the shoulder. Then I hurried to the clubhouse to find my girl.

Kiara curled up on a couch in the lounge, sketching, while Cat watched over her from behind the bar. When she saw me, she leaned over and said something to Kiara whose head whipped up and looked around. She spotted me, and a beautiful smile lit up her face.

"Sometimes I can't fucking believe I get to come home to this for the rest of my life," I mumbled as I ambled up to where she was sitting. Kiara was more than anything I could have ever wished for, and I knew I would spend every day protecting her and making her smile. And someday, I'd make the same vow for each of our children.

"You were gone longer than I expected, did you get what you needed?"

I plucked her up and took her seat, then settled her in my lap. "Yeah, baby. I got everything I needed."

11

KIARA

After Shane told me about his meeting with Bickle, it took a little time for it to sink in. I was nervous about calling my dad to tell him that the guy wouldn't be a problem anymore. Although it was great news, I knew he would push hard for me to come home, and that was the last thing I wanted. I was still beyond angry with my dad for what he'd done. And I was so happy with Shane. I didn't want anything to come between us or spoil our first holiday together.

Almost as though he could sense that I was considering how long I could put off making that call, my phone rang and I saw his picture on the screen when I pulled it out of my pocket. Heaving a deep sigh, I tapped my finger against the green button and answered, "Hey, Dad. You must've heard me thinking about you. I wanted to tell you that the Silver Saints made a deal with that Bickle guy and—"

He interrupted me to say, "I know, Kiara. He just called."

My back straightened at his abrupt tone as fear seeped in that he was going to be a jerk now that his problem had been taken care of. "Oh, well then I guess you already know the good news."

"I wish I could agree that it was good, but what Bickle had to say to me was the exact opposite."

My brows drew together, and my head jerked up as I jumped off Shane's lap. He followed me as I switched to speaker mode. "I don't understand. How could it be bad that Bickle agreed to stay away from our family? That's what we wanted."

"I...have no idea how the hell I'm supposed to tell you this so I can soften the blow."

My body tensed at his anguished tone as I considered how enormous the last secret he'd kept from me had been. Shane took the phone from my trembling fingers and pulled me into his arms as Cash and Mac strode over to see what was happening. "Just say it. I'm here to make sure she can handle whatever the hell it is this time."

"There isn't anything else," my dad swore.

"Quit stalling and spit it out. You're just making this harder on Kiara," Shane growled.

"The deal you made with Bickle didn't cover Karina."

I lifted my face from where I'd buried it against Shane's chest to gawk at the phone. "Who is that? I don't know anyone named Karina."

There was a long pause before he answered, "Your sister."

My eyes widened as my breath caught in my lungs. "I don't have a sister."

"I'm so sorry, Kiara. I didn't want you to find out this way. Karina is your half sister. I didn't think Bickle would discover she existed, but I have another daughter."

My knees buckled as my vision darkened, and Shane's embrace was the only thing that stopped me from falling to the floor. Cash took the phone from him so he could sweep me into his arms and carry me back over to the couch where we'd been sitting. Dropping onto the cushion, he cuddled me against his chest while I tried to wrap my head around what my dad had just confessed. "How old is she?" I finally whispered.

Cash had followed us, along with Mac, so my

dad was able to hear my question. "A year younger than you."

Learning that he had kept such a huge secret for so long tore my heart to shreds. I'd known that my parents weren't happy together, but I never would have suspected my dad cheated on her. "Are there any other surprise siblings out there that I should know about?"

My dad sighed. "No, just Karina. Her mom couldn't have any more children after we had her."

The way he worded that made me wonder if he had an actual relationship with the woman and it hadn't been just a fling that had burned out years ago. "Are you still with her? Have you been keeping a second family from me?"

"I couldn't just leave Karina's mom. Stephanie is...well, everything your mom isn't. When I'm with her, I feel free. I couldn't let that go, even though I've known all this time that what I was doing was wrong."

His explanation didn't make me feel any better. "I know things aren't great between you and Mom and she can be a lot, but how could you do this to her? To me?"

"I'm so sorry, sweetie. Please know that what I've done doesn't mean I don't love you. The only reason

I didn't leave your mom was because you mean the world to me, and I couldn't do that to you. No matter how much I love Stephanie."

He really had a whole other family I never knew about. "I'm guessing all those judicial conferences and fishing trips were time you spent with her? Does she know about me? Or have you been lying to her for her entire life too?"

"This is going to come as much of a shock to her as it is to you."

I took some small comfort in the fact that the sister I'd never known would be going through the same upheaval as me. Maybe our anger at my...*our* dad would bring us together, like a weird bonding experience.

So many questions swirled in my head, but I couldn't bring myself to ask any of them. I didn't want to hear any of his excuses. Not after everything he'd done.

Tilting my face up to look at Shane, I shook my head as a tear trickled down my cheek. He pressed a kiss to my forehead before turning to Mac. "We gotta step in and make sure her sister is safe."

"Damn straight." Jerking his chin toward Cash, he demanded, "Take one of the SUVs and head over to the judge's house to get all the information on the girl. Then go get her and bring her back here while we hunt for Bickle."

"I'll be ready with everything you need," my dad confirmed before hanging up.

"No wonder Bickle agreed to the deal so easily," Shane muttered. "He had to have known about her already."

"The bastard is gonna pay for trying to pull a fast one over on the Silver Saints," Mac vowed.

Staring up at Shane, I asked, "After all the trouble you guys have already gone through because of my father, why would you do this for me?"

"Haven't you figured it out yet, baby?" He cradled me closer against his chest. "I'd do anything for you."

"You've already more than proven that, but I don't understand why," I admitted.

"Because you're mine, Kiara." There was no missing the emotion shining from his blue orbs as he added, "I love you."

"You do?" I sniffled, the tears welling in my eyes changing from shocked to happy at his gruff confession.

"Never would've claimed you as mine in every way I could if I didn't," he confirmed.

My lips curved as I thought about all the times

that he'd called me his. I never should've doubted how much he'd meant it. "I love you, too,"

"You'd better." His hand dropped down to cup my belly. "Because I'm pretty damn sure you're already carrying my baby."

"What?" I shook my head, my eyes widening. "No."

"Baby." He chuckled and shook his head. "You've been tired as fuck and had morning sickness the past few days. I've been around enough of my brothers' women when they were knocked up to know those are sure signs of pregnancy, and I've damn well done my best to make sure you were."

My cheeks heated as I thought about how true that statement was. "Um, well...yeah. But you really think I'm pregnant?"

"I do." He stood with me in his arms, hugging me close before he gently set me on my feet. "But the only way we'll know for sure is if you take a test. You can sure as fuck use some good news after the shit your dad just laid on you, so I'll run out and grab one now."

"No need. I already sent out an SOS." I'd somehow totally forgotten we weren't alone. My head jerked back, and I turned to stare at Mac. "Patch finally wised up and started keeping them in stock when he got Willa pregnant. He's gonna bring one over for you."

I shook my head and laughed so hard that tears streamed down my cheeks and I couldn't catch my breath. I'd just gone through a roller coaster of emotions in a short time, not to mention I almost definitely had pregnancy hormones coursing through my body. So this small thing was enough to make me lose it, but in the best way possible.

When my laughter finally ended, Shane brushed his fingers against my cheeks to wipe the tears away. "You okay, baby?"

I nodded. "Yeah, sorry. That was just too hilarious."

"Not sure what was so damn funny," Mac muttered, earning him a glare from Shane at his disgruntled tone.

I loved how protective Shane was over me, but it wasn't necessary with his president. Mac had never been anything but kind to me, and I had just laughed my butt off over something he'd said.

Twisting around, I offered him a soft smile. "Sorry, it just struck me as super funny that your club doctor has a supply of pregnancy tests. It's the last thing anyone would ever expect from a motorcycle club, but I shouldn't have been surprised. One thing I've learned in the past couple of weeks is that the Silver Saints do whatever it takes to make sure their women have what they need."

"Damn straight," Mac agreed with a nod.

"Always gonna take care of you, baby," Shane confirmed.

Although I was still struggling with my dad's betrayals, I had no doubt that was true. Not just because Shane had shown me that I came first for him...but also because I'd seen how his club brothers treated their women. Any woman lucky enough to get claimed by a Silver Saint had a lifetime of love and happiness to look forward to.

EPILOGUE

Kiara's laughter drew my attention, and I stopped focusing on what Mac was telling me so I could listen to the musical sound. She was sitting at the bar talking to Cat, giving me a great view of her incredible ass, and her pretty blond hair hung down her back in soft waves.

Fuck, my woman is gorgeous.

But the best part was the large patch on her back that deemed her my property. It was as important to me as the ring I'd slipped on her finger the day after I'd made a deal with the devil to keep her safe.

"Knight," Mac grunted.

I swung my gaze back to him and shrugged unapologetically.

"Cash sent word. He found the sister and is

bringing her back here."

We didn't bring every person we rescued to the compound. Otherwise, it would be crowded and feel like the revolving door to a hotel. Instead, we had safe houses and arrangements with local motels and shelters. However, there was no fucking way that I was gonna entrust the safety of my old lady's sister to anyone else, and the two women needed a chance to meet and get to know each other.

Karina had been out of town when Cash first went to retrieve her. Apparently, she'd graduated early, and her parents had gifted her a ski trip in the mountains over Christmas. She was in Aspen with her mom, and Timkins had planned to join them on Christmas Day. So Cash had to haul his ass all the way out to Aspen and bring her back. It would have been just as easy for Bickle to get to her there.

"Were there any complications? I expected him to be back before Christmas."

Mac grunted again and folded his arms across his chest. "The judge called and warned Karina's mom that we were coming for her daughter. It took some convincing for her to agree. But it seems Karina had to be convinced as well. She had a tough time believing her dad could do any of these things."

I couldn't blame her. My girl had struggled with

the knowledge that the loving, attentive father she knew had turned out to be a lying, crooked, cheating asshole.

"He got tired of asking and snatched her."

A bark of laughter escaped my chest, and I saw Kiara glance back at me with a happy smile. I winked, and she blushed prettily before returning to her conversation with Cat.

The front door suddenly slammed open, and a tiny woman who bore a stark resemblance to my woman came marching inside. Cash ambled in after her, looking at ease, but I could see the tension vibrating in him, and his alert gaze never left the young woman.

"He tell her about Kiara?" I queried.

"Timkins told her she existed, but nothing else."

"I want to speak to whoever is in charge!" Karina demanded, planting her hands on her hips. As I walked over to Kiara, I had to swallow a laugh because Karina looked so much like her sister on the day she pulled up to the compound.

"Relax, sunshine," Cash muttered. "You'll get your questions answered, just like I promised. For now, let's get you settled."

Kiara was leaning against me, holding her breath, every muscle in her body tense.

"Want me to take care of her until you're ready to meet?" Cat offered softly.

When Kiara didn't respond, I simply nodded and offered Cat a grateful smile.

She sauntered over to the new arrivals with a welcoming smile.

"You must be Karina. I'm Cat, your tour guide and safety director. If you follow me, I'll take you to your room." Before turning away, Cat shot Cash a questioning glance, and he nodded.

Hmm...well, this was bound to be interesting.

"What was that?" Kiara asked when she finally found her voice.

"What, baby?"

"That." She pointed at Cash, and I looked down to see her face scrunched in consternation. "He's staring at my sister. And what was all that silent communication with Cat—" She broke off with a gasp. "He is not putting my sister in his room!"

Before I could stop her, she was marching toward him. "What do you think you're doing, Cash?" she snapped.

He turned to glare at her but pulled it back slightly when he saw the expression on my face. If he so much as raised his voice to my woman, we were gonna have a problem.

Kiara wagged her finger at him and continued, "You can't—"

"Baby," I interrupted once I caught up with her. I tucked her under my arm and bent my head to whisper in her ear. "You can't get involved."

"But—"

"If he's decided that she's his, we will not get involved," I said more firmly. "Promise me."

She glared at Cash's back as he stalked out of the room. "They just met," she hissed.

I trailed my lips across her jaw and back to place a kiss on the sensitive skin under her ear. She shivered, and I grinned at her reaction as I murmured, "How long had you known me before you let me inside your sweet pussy, baby?"

Her skin flushed a pretty shade of pink, and she licked her lips, sending blood rushing to my cock.

"I knew instantly that you were mine."

"It doesn't always happen like that," she protested.

"When a Silver Saint finds his woman, there is no timeline, baby. We see what's meant to be ours, and we fucking take it. We fall hard, love harder, and knock her up as soon as possible." I grinned at the last part as my hands settled over her tummy.

"You think he really fell for her?" she inquired

softly.

I'd recognized the look in his eyes. One I'd seen in many of my brothers'...and in my own. "Yup."

"Well..." She harrumphed a little, then continued, "Doesn't look like she's going to make it easy on him. At least it'll be fun to watch."

"You're underestimating the determination and animal instincts of a Silver Saint, baby. But"—I swept her up into my arms and made my way to the back door, heading to our apartment—"I'm more than happy to demonstrate it so you remember."

Kiara giggled and put her arms around my neck before laying her head under my chin. "Will he love her?"

"Fiercely."

"Like you love me?"

I stopped and waited until she lifted her head and met my gaze. "I don't think anyone could love another person as much as I love you, baby. But I'm sure he'll come close."

"I love you, too, Shane," she sighed, brushing a kiss over my lips.

"I love it when you call me Shane, baby," I growled as I hurried up the stairs to the apartment. "Let's see how many times I can make you scream it before dinner."

EPILOGUE
KIARA

"I can't believe I'm really having an exhibit dedicated to my artwork." I turned in a full circle, staring in awe at the walls of the small gallery. My drawings hung in beautiful frames with lights shining on each piece.

"They were lucky to snap you up. You're fucking amazing."

I beamed a smile at my husband. Keegan, our youngest at only two months old, was strapped to his chest. Carrying our babies like that didn't take away from his masculinity at all. If anything, it had the opposite effect of making my ovaries spontaneously combust...which was probably why we'd had three children in only five years. Kaylee and Kennedy were a few doors down from the art gallery, having a scoop at the ice cream shop with Molly—Mac and Bridget's eldest daughter. With two in diapers and one almost ready for kindergarten, I'd learned that people were right when they said it took a village to raise children. And I had the best one—the Silver Saints.

Leaning closer, I brushed a kiss against the top of our son's head. "Was that your pitch when you talked to them?"

He flashed me a sexy grin. "I toned down my language some because I didn't want to scare the fuck outta the owner, but yeah."

"Thank you for believing in me."

I'd been stunned when Shane had told me a few months ago that he'd brought his favorite pieces of mine to a gallery, and they were interested in them. I was even more shocked when we met with the owner, who offered me a solo exhibit. That was unusual for an unknown artist, but he insisted that my work didn't need to hang with other artists to bring people into the gallery.

"How could I not, baby? I've hiked my prices five times since you've been helping me with the designs, and my waitlist is still fucking ridiculous."

I rolled my eyes at his compliment. "Only because you're the best swordsmith out there."

"Not gonna deny that"—he swayed side to side as Keegan started to fuss—"but the number of clients I have waiting for shit has more than doubled since you started drawing for me. Your art combined with my forging skills is a killer combo, baby."

"Well, hopefully my work does as well on its own." I padded over to the nearest drawing and traced my fingers over the card beneath it. "I still can't believe he's charging so much."

"And I still think he could have upped the price," Shane muttered.

I rolled my eyes with a giggle. "Only because you're biased."

"Hell yeah, I am," he agreed with a grin. "But that doesn't mean I'm wrong."

I smoothed my hands down the skirt of my dress. "I just want this show to be a success."

"I have no doubt it will be, but you're already a success, baby." He wrapped his fingers around my wrist and lifted my left hand to kiss my knuckle above where his rings rested. "The best wife and mother a man could ask for. A fucking amazing artist who not only has done a shit ton of kick-ass designs for me but also has a bunch of people walking around with her art on their bodies. Including me."

I loved how much faith Shane had in me and

how he always gave me his unconditional support. When we first got together, he'd even offered to move to my college town until I was ready to graduate. It would've meant three and a half years away from his club, but he hadn't even hesitated.

That he was so willing to make a sacrifice like that meant the world to me, but dropping out had been an easy decision for me to make, with or without the pregnancy. I'd only gone to college in the first place because I hadn't wanted to disappoint my dad. But after everything he'd done, I had refused to allow his expectations to dictate my future. My art was my passion, and I didn't need a degree to pursue it. Not when I had two thriving businesses vying to use my designs.

It had taken some finagling to get Shane to agree to my drawing for Silver Ink too. He was greedy for my time and attention and didn't like to share me with anyone, but he caved when he realized how excited I was to do some tattoo designs...as long as he got first dibs on anything that wasn't a special request. The man went from having no ink to proudly showing off the ten he'd gotten over the nearly six years we'd been together.

Stroking my fingers down his back, I beamed a soft smile at him as I traced the lines I could see beneath his shirt. I knew them by heart. His first tattoo, one I'd drawn especially for him...a visual representation of how much I loved him. "Don't be surprised if I hit the studio when we get home tonight."

My warning wasn't really needed since I spent a lot of my free time in the large studio Shane had built on the property we'd bought after buying our home. "Feeling inspired by seeing your artwork displayed like this?"

"Nope." I went up on my toes to brush my lips against his, careful not to disturb Keegan. "Just like every day since we met, my love for you is my biggest and best inspiration."

Curious about what happens with Cash and Karina? Their story (Cash) is up next!

If you sign up for our newsletter, you'll get an email from us with a link to claim a free copy of The Virgin's Guardian, which is no longer available to purchase.

ABOUT THE AUTHOR

The writing duo of Elle Christensen and Rochelle Paige team up under the Fiona Davenport pen name to bring you sexy, insta-love stories filled with alpha males. If you want a quick & dirty read with a guaranteed happily ever after, then give Fiona Davenport a try!

Don't miss out on new release news and giveaways; sign up for our newsletter!

Printed in Dunstable, United Kingdom

<u>Contents</u>

Forward

There are great difficulties about writing true crime stories as there is an importance in keeping them as accurate to the truth as possible yet protecting the people involved. The stories are based on the true facts of several cases but with no details of the offenders and some locations changed. I have done this as the true names do not alter the facts of the cases, but I accept that it is possible that some of these people may have changed and moved on in their lives and nothing is gained by them being identified. I made the decision to protect their privacy.

The facts were obtained from my own memories having worked on the cases told in this book. I lived the jobs for many months and spoke directly to most of the people connected to the case.